About the Author

My name is Bryn William Hopkins. I was born in 1975 to James and Linda Hopkins. I was introduced to the world of reading by my older brother, Gary, who handed me a book by David Gemmel, at the age of eighteen. I have struggled with reading all my life, as I'm severely dyslexic, and never really enjoyed reading. After twenty years of reading novels, I decided to have a go at my own story, and found it most enjoyable. This book took me around six months to write. I hope you enjoy reading this, as much as I enjoyed writing it.

The Hunted

Bryn Hopkins

The Hunted

Olympia Publishers
London

First Published in 2022

Olympia Publishers
Tallis House
2 Tallis Street
London
EC4Y 0AB

Printed in Great Britain

Dedication

I dedicate this book to my loving wife, Andria Hopkins, who has been a constant support to me through our life together.

Acknowledgements

To my son, Regan, and my younger brother, Darryl, a special thanks to you two. As I based the main character, Wil, on both of you, my son is the hulking power house and my brother is a martial arts instructor. Also, I would like to thank my youngest daughter, Deren, your independence in life gave me the idea for the character, Vanessa. And a special mention to my eldest daughter, Melissa, who always believed in me.

Prologue
SCOTTISH HIGHLANDS

The silence of the highlands was broken by a thunderous bang and a flash of bright light, the falling object came hurtling from the sky, the impact drove it hard into the ground, huge amounts of soil were thrown into the air, trees were up rooted as the ship came to rest in the woods. Inside the craft the Mojave pilot had been pinned to his seat by a piece of the ship that had skewered through his reptilian body, his life's blood running out.

Clinging to life the Mojave pilot tried to move, pain lanced through him causing him to cry out, his silted eyes caught movement in the shadows. A huge hulking beast with black shiny skin and six limbs moved towards him, its powerful front legs pushing aside pieces of the ship that blocked its path, franticly he reached for his weapon trying to aim at the creature moving towards him, he pulled the trigger, nothing happened. The energy core was smashed, the weapon useless. The Mojave pilot looked into the eyes of death as the creature lowered its head down, its hot breath filled the nostrils of the pilot who was now breathing heavy. Two small arms unfolded from beneath the powerful front legs, the small claw-like hand flexing as it reached out and grabbed the pilot's head. The pilot tried to pull his head back but the arms held his head in place, the creature opened its beak-like mouth and let out a terrible growl. The creature was up on him before he could scream, ripping him to pieces. The creature turned and let out a grunting sound, which was answered. Slowly two creatures made their way through the wrecked ship. In the dark of the night two huge black forms emerged sniffing the air, new scent filling their nostrils, a low growl came from the larger of two creatures and they both moved off into the distance.

Chapter One

Angus pulled up to the farmhouse and turned off the engine of the quad, Morag was stood in the doorway to the house smiling at him. Angus, now in his late sixties and still powerfully built, returned the warm smile from his wife. "And what are you up to on that thing, you old fool?" asked Morag. She was a pretty woman in her mid-fifties, slightly plump but carried the weight well.

"I thought we could take a ride up to the cabin and get it ready for Wil and his friends. Maybe take a picnic with us and enjoy the sunshine and the fresh air?" said Angus.

Morag gave out a small chuckle. "And what makes you think I have nothing better to do than go for a picnic?" replied Morag.

Angus spread his hands out. "Well not just a picnic, I could show you that there is still life in this old fool, and if you're nice to me you could be in for a treat," he said.

Morag laughed aloud. "Well since you put it like that how can I refuse? I'll go and pack some things together," she said. Turning she headed back inside the house.

Taking a deep breath Angus looked round the now empty farm yard, his thoughts were of the farm in its heyday when his father had had one of the biggest dairy herds in the highlands. "What do I know about farming?"

he said to himself. "I've been in the army since I was sixteen. I'm a military man not a farmer."

Morag's voice cut through his day dreaming. "Who are you talking to love?" she said.

"No one my dear," replied Angus. "I was just wishing that the farm had prospered the same as when my father ran it."

"Hush now," said Morag. "You did your best, no one could have foreseen the prices dropping like they did. You've given it your best shot at least with the sale of the herds and some of the land we're going to be okay."

Angus took a deep breath. "I wish I'd had more time to fix it, make things right. I know I have no kids to leave the farm to but it's been in my family for three generations." The words came out before he could stop them and he saw the pain on Morag's face. "I'm sorry lass, I didn't mean it like that," he said.

Morag held out her hand to him. "I would have loved to have given you sons and daughters," she said. "But the lord saw fit not to bless us with wee ones." Taking hold of her hand he raised it to his lips and kissed it.

"I would not have it any other way, my love, I would live a hundred lifetimes with you. Besides I will leave the farm to William and Vanessa, it will be theirs to do as they please once we are gone," he said.

Sweeping her up into his arms and kissing her, Morag let out a laugh. "Put me down you old fool, you'll put your back out," she said. "Go grab the stuff from the kitchen and let's be off."

Angus did as he was bid and came from the house carrying the picnic Morag had prepared. In his hand he had a shotgun. Morag looked at him. "What are you doing with that?" she asked.

"It's for Wil," he replied. "Now that he's nineteen I think he should have it, this is the gun that Wil's dad saved my life with."

"I know that!" she said. "I've heard the story a thousand times now. Let's head out, I'm looking forward to this picnic. Angus started the quad and he and Morag set off into the highlands leaving the deserted farm.

Angus lay on the blanket, Morag by his side, gently rubbing her fingers through his chest hair. "Now that was a treat," she said.

Coming up on to his elbow he kissed her. "I love you, lass," he told her.

"I know you do, you big lump," said Morag. "When are Wil and Vanessa due to arrive?" Angus was stock still, his eyes narrowed. "Are you listening to me Angus?" said Morag.

"Hush now woman" he snapped.

Morag whispered, "What is it? What's wrong?"

"Listen," said Angus.

Morag lay there, listening. After a few seconds saying, "I don't hear anything."

"No, neither do I. No bird song. Nothing... Something isn't right," said Angus.

"Get dressed."

Standing, he took the shotgun from the back of the quad. "Hurry lass, I have a bad feeling."

"I'm moving as quick as I can," said Morag, placing their things on the quad. Angus placed the gun back on the quad securing it, Morag climbed on behind him and

Angus started the engine. From behind them came a crashing sound as bushes exploded. A huge black form came charging at them. Angus set off at speed, Morag let out a cry of pain as the quad sped off. The huge creature stood watching, as its prey sped away. Lifting up its huge paw it smelt the blood, a forked tongue licked at the blood on one of the razor-sharp talons. The beast quivered with delight as the new taste filled its mouth, with a sway of its head it set off in the same direction as the quad.

At nineteen years old, Wil Jameson was an impressive young man. At six feet two inches and weighing nearly eighteen stone, the young powerhouse walked down the corridor towards the exit, all around him students were laughing and making their way out of the building. A few of the girl students waved at him as he walked past them. He was a handsome young man with dark brown eyes and shoulder length hair pulled back in a ponytail and shaved at the sides. Another term of college was over and Wil was looking forward to his trip away from all the bustle and stress of college life. He had always been a serious young man — a strict upbringing from his father had taught him discipline at a young age. Not only had Wil been subject to army rules, his father had pushed Wil to his physical limits. The young man had been taken out into the wilderness along with his twin sister Vanessa and there they had been left to find their way back to the remote cabin. At nineteen years old he could read animal trails, hunt from the land for his food and was well diverse in multiple self-defence techniques. He had thought on many occasions that his father had been hard on him and his sister but looking back he now knew that this was all a life lesson preparing him for manhood.

As he opened the doors at the end of the corridor, coming out onto the steps he paused to take a deep breath, from his left a familiar voice called his name. "Hey there, little Willy," said Vanessa in a mocking tone.

Wil looked at his sister and smiled, Vanessa was a stunning looking woman. At five foot eight inches tall she had an athletic build, shoulder length brown hair and dark brown eyes. "Nessy," shouted Wil, returning the greeting. Taking the steps two at a time he ran down and picked up his sister in a huge bear hug. "How many times have I asked you not to call me Willy?" he said, placing his sister back on the floor.

Laughing, she replied, "About the same number of times I've asked you to stop calling me Nessy!"

"How long have you been waiting out here?" he asked his sister.

"Not long, only twenty minutes. I finished work early so I could meet you and take my baby brother home from school," she said teasing him.

"You're five minutes older than me," he replied.

"And don't you forget that," added Vanessa. Smiling he placed his arm around her shoulder.

"I hope you're as happy to see me," said a voice from behind them. Turning Wil saw his girlfriend, Rochelle, walking towards them, a look of suspicion on her face.

Wil stepped forward and kissed Rochelle, she backed away smiling and looked at Vanessa. "Are you going to introduce me to your friend?" she asked him.

Pushing past her brother Vanessa exclaimed, "I'm

Vanessa, Wil's twin sister." Taking hold of Rochelle in an embrace, "You will have to excuse my brother, the socially awkward one, he never was very good around girls."

"That's true," replied Rochelle.

"Wow," said Vanessa. "Wil said you were beautiful but he didn't do you justice!"

"Thank you," answered Rochelle, blushing. "He told me he had a twin sister but never mentioned how beautiful you were."

"That's my baby brother for you. A man of very few words."

Both women stood looking at Wil who started to feel uncomfortable. He was glad to see his friend approaching. With a loud belch in Vanessa's ear Tom came and eased his friends' uncomfortable tension as the focus was drawn to him. "Ladies," said Tom with an elaborate bow. "So nice to see you." Tom was a handsome young man of average height and build, who's laughter was so infectious that people instinctively warmed to him. He greeted Wil with a high five. "Man, I'm so ready for this trip. College is done for six weeks and I get to chill out with Mary."

Rochelle looked at Wil asking, "So, where are you taking me? I hope it's some place warm."

Looking at his girlfriend, Wil told her, "We're off to Scotland, to my dad's cabin. We'll drive up there, do some hiking and some camping, live off the land, no internet, no mobile phone signal, completely off the grid."

Stepping back Rochelle looked at Wil. "Take a look

at me," she said. "Tell me what you see."

Tom quickly interrupted, "Wil don't answer that, it's a trick question!"

"Shut up Tom," snapped Rochelle. Still looking at Wil she asked again. "Well, what do you see?"

Uncomfortable now, Wil looked back at her. "Err, I see my beautiful girlfriend?" he stammered.

Vanessa started to laugh. "Wow! Good answer baby bro." Wil gave his sister a warning look as Vanessa moved to Rochelle's side.

Smiling now Rochelle asked, "Well, what do you see? What colour is my skin?"

Wil looked at Rochelle. She was five foot seven, had brown golden skin with shoulder length wavy black hair. "It's brown," he answered smiling.

"So, does that tell you that I come from exotic stock and I like warm places? Where I can swim in clear blue oceans and drink ice cold cocktails?"

Wil looked back at his girlfriend and with a straight face replied, "Babe you're from Leeds. So are both your parents. You were born here in England."

Rochelle let out a huge sigh. "I give up," she said throwing up her hands. "Well, I suppose I will have to save that new bikini for another time."

Tom burst out laughing and patted his friend on the back. "Dude, you really are clueless when it comes to women."

"Okay, that's enough embarrassment for my brother," interrupted Vanessa. "Let's get going. We'll all meet at Wil's in the morning, John will pick us up from there."

As Vanessa and Rochelle headed off to Vanessa's car, Tom grabbed Wil by the arm. "Dude, your sister's boyfriend is coming on this trip. Why?"

Wil looked at his friend. "Don't worry," replied Wil. "I'll handle John. I'll make sure he doesn't upset anyone."

Tom looked at his friend thinking, "You could handle most things my friend, but John is a dick and I'm afraid you could seriously hurt him if you lost control." Smiling he said, "Okay man, but you know that Brad hates John and won't be happy."

"Don't worry about Brad, he'll be fine."

Tom looked at his friend. "Okay dude, if you say so. I'll be at yours bright and early." The two friends shook hands and Tom turned and walked off in the opposite direction. Tom was right, John was a dick and could be a problem. Wil knew why Brad hated John. Brad had been in love with Vanessa ever since they were kids but never had the courage to tell her. It all started when Brad was ten, he had fallen out of a tree, breaking his wrist. He had cried screaming for his mother but the kids had all been at least a half mile from the house. Vanessa had calmed Brad down by talking to him while Wil had set off at speed to fetch one of their parents. It wasn't long before Wil came running back with his father. Vanessa had made a makeshift splint out of her socks and some tree branches. Brad had been sat calmly as Wil's father approached, his chubby little face smeared by his tears.

"Now young Brad, let's have a look at you," said Wil's father. Brad had lifted his arm showing the makeshift splint Vanessa had applied.

"It hurts Mr Jameson," said Brad holding back his tears.

"I bet it does. Let's be getting you back home and then to hospital. Your mother is going frantic with worry." Alex Jameson had carried Brad back home and had taken him to hospital along with his mother,

When he had arrived home, his children had been sat waiting, wanting to know how Brad was. "He'll be fine," he told the twins. "The break was a clean one," said their father. "That splint you applied saved him a lot of pain. Nice to see you're listening and learning what I show you."

Wil looked at his father. "I told him not to climb the tree, Dad, but he wanted to show Nessy he could do it."

"Don't call me Nessy! I hate it!" she snapped at her brother.

Vanessa asked her father, "Can we go and see him? Please Dad!"

Alex looked at his children and smiled. "Yes, go and see him. But don't be long, your dinners will be on the table in an hour."

Brad, his face still tear-stained, proudly showed off the plaster cast on his arm. Vanessa had taken the marker pen and in big letters wrote "get better soon, love Ness" with three large XXXs for kisses. It was from that point on that Brad's infatuation of Vanessa had started. No one else had been allowed to write on the cast.

A horn sounded, snapping Wil out of his daydream. "Are you coming or what baby bro?" shouted his sister. Smiling, Wil walked over to the car.

Rochelle and Vanessa were in deep conversation

when Wil got to the car. "Vanessa was just telling me about her job. How she gets to visit all the different countries and how she can be gone for a couple of months at a time!"

"That's my sister for you," answered Wil. "The jet-setting hotel life, never in one spot for too long, hey sis."

"The pay is good," she answered. "And someone has to pay the bills while you're doing your studies."

Wil smiled at his sister. "I'm hungry, let's go eat!"

Rochelle shook her head. "You, my love, are always hungry."

Wil dropped the heavy dumbbells to the floor, sweat running down his body. This was his preferred method of stress relief. All tension seemed to be stripped away in the gym, his father had built the gym at home converting the garage. Wil had soon started to gain muscle under his father's tuition. At fourteen, Wil had been one of the tallest in his class, his father had pushed Wil in the gym five days a week allowing him two days of rest. His father's words echoed in his mind, "There is no point in training tired muscle, boy. You'll do more harm than good; the body needs time to repair. Always remember that."

Wil had lived by his father's teachings his entire life. Now his father was gone, struck down by a brain aneurysm. The death of his father one and a half years ago had hit both of them hard. His sister had taken the job that had taken her all over the world, leaving Wil on his own, only seeing his sister every few months when she had the time to stop by. Tom and Brad were his best friends, more like family now. They had all remembered

Wil's father with fondness, one night Tom had asked about Wil's mother, but Wil's answer had shocked his friends. "I don't remember her is the truth. She died when I was a toddler, killed in a car crash. Dad loved her, I know that. He never had another woman in his life that I know of. He just raised Ness and me. The man never showed much emotion, only on a few rare occasions. He only ever praised us when we learnt a new skill or when he came back after a mission."

Returning the weights to the rack he placed his earphones in and put on the boxing gloves. The bag was heavy and Wil started slowly jabbing at the bag, picking up speed as he went along. Harder and faster, punch after punch, then elbow strikes followed by kicks, the power and speed growing with every strike. Finally exhausted and covered in sweat, he pulled off the gloves and removed the earphones. Taking in a huge breath and slowly stretching out his muscles, he was completely unaware of Rochelle watching him. Only when she spoke, was he aware of her being there.

"I hope you have some energy left for tonight," she said huskily. Wil jumped which made her chuckle. "You could have skipped the workout. Missing one day wouldn't hurt you and I'd love a work out later if you know what I mean."

She was wearing one of his t-shirts, leaning on the door frame her legs were bare and Wil could see her nipples protruding through the thin t-shirt. He smiled at her. "It's like my father always said, 'no one else can do the work for you and what doesn't kill you will only make you stronger'."

Rochelle could see the pain in his eyes as he mentioned his father. "You miss him, don't you?" she said.

"Not a single day goes by that I wouldn't give anything just to hear his voice again and sit and talk with him," he replied.

Stepping towards him she ran her hand over his massive chest, she looked up into his dark brown eyes, such pain there. But also, she could see the love in his eyes that he felt for her, Rochelle took a step backwards. "You need a shower, you're so sweaty and you stink!"

Wil reached out and grabbed hold of the front of her t-shirt pulling her back towards him with a mischievous smile on his face. Rochelle let out a playful scream.

"No!" said Rochelle. "Don't you dare!" Wil said nothing and slowly pulled her forward. "I mean it Wil, don't you dare!" she said again, smiling at him. Wil looked at her with a mischievous grin. "No!" she said again, trying not to laugh. "Don't you dare!"

"Give me a kiss," he said. Then without another word Wil took hold of Rochelle and embraced her in a huge hug. His powerful arms encircling her, leaning down he kissed her. She had started to struggle but as soon as his lips met hers it ceased, the kiss was long and deep. In that moment Rochelle knew that she was safe in his arms and that the love she felt for this man was real. Wil slowly moved his head back, looking at the woman in his arms, gently he reached up and stroked her cheek with the back of his fingers. "You're so beautiful," he told her.

She smiled back at him. "Now I'm all sweaty," she said, pouting her lips. "Well, I'll be in the shower if you care to join me." She winked at him turned and walked straight out of the gym without another word. Wil quickly placed the gym equipment back and set off to join Rochelle in the shower.

Wil came into the bedroom, his towel wrapped round his waist he looked down at the bed. Rochelle had once again stolen his favourite t-shirt using it as a nightshirt. Wil recalled the day they had first met. He had been at the gym, lost in a world of his own training when he saw four women enter. Rochelle had stood out to him instantly — her long dark hair pulled back into a ponytail, the warmth of her smile, her golden-brown skin. She had looked over at him and giggled, a flush of embarrassment had caused him to redden. Quickly he had looked away and continued his work out. For over an hour Wil could feel the gaze of the four women upon him. He had tried not to look but something about this girl stirred deep within him. They had left and Wil relaxed. He had never been very good around women, always feeling shy. He placed the dumbbells back on the rack and walked over to the reception area where old Jack was sat with his feet upon the desk. "Who were the four women that came in?" Wil asked.

Old Jack gave a crooked smile. "Which one caught your eye?" he said.

Wil blushed. "None in particular. I just noticed that they were new."

"Shame," said old Jack. "The black girl couldn't stop talking about you to her friends."

"Really?" asked Wil.

Old Jack laughed and winked. "I thought you didn't

notice anyone in particular?" Wil blushed again. "Don't worry lad, your secret is safe with me. I have a feeling she'll be back just to see you… Her name is Rochelle by the way," added Jack. "If you're interested."

For the next week Wil had awkwardly looked over at Rochelle and her friends trying to think of something to say but could never find the words. The week after she had turned up but only one of her friends had come with her. More confident now, Wil had gone over to the two women who were in the middle of their workout. "Would you mind if I offer some advice?" he asked them.

The two women looked and smiled at him. "No, we wouldn't," answered Rochelle.

"Spread your legs a little further apart. That will stop you from engaging your back in the exercise. If you carry on doing as you are that could cause you to injure your back by pulling a muscle," he told them.

The other woman looked at Wil and asked, "Is that how you talk to all the woman here? You ask them to spread their legs for you?" Then she burst out laughing.

Wil blushed and walked away. He heard Rochelle asking her friend, "Why did you say that? He's only trying to be nice."

"I was just teasing him. I'd like to pull his muscles," she said.

The next day Wil stood in the gym waiting for Rochelle to arrive, determined to talk with her. He had a joke prepared, hoping this would make her laugh and then the conversation would start. Wil heard the laughter coming from the gym entrance and then he saw her. She was dressed in black and pink lycra that enhanced her body even more. Her long black hair had been pulled back into a ponytail, the two-piece outfit showing off her flat stomach and her ample breast stood out in the sports bra top. His mouth went dry as she walked in. With his heart pounding in his chest, he headed over towards the two women.

"Hi there," he managed to say. "I'm sorry if what I said yesterday caused embarrassment for either of you, I was only offering advice."

Rochelle stepped in front of her friend and smiled back at him. "No offence taken, my friend here was only teasing, weren't you Jess. Before Jess could say a word Rochelle added, "We're doing something called a dead lift. Would you mind watching to make sure we do it right?"

"Sure," said Wil. "Let's get set up, then we can start." He cleared his throat. "Would you like to hear a joke?" he asked them both.

"I would love to," answered Rochelle.

Wil cleared his throat again. "Why did the blonde girl stare at the carton of orange juice?" Rochelle shrugged. "Because it said concentrate," said Wil.

Rochelle's laughter had been music to his ears. The joke wasn't that funny but she had laughed and laughed, grabbing hold of Wil's arm and squeezing his bicep.

He started instructing them on the deadlift. He couldn't help but look at the shape of Rochelle's hips in the tight lycra leggings. She bent over to lower the bar to the floor, with Wil stood behind her she stumbled backwards. Wil caught her. "Are you okay," he asked.

She turned to face him, putting her hand on his chest,

she felt him tense. Looking into his eyes she whispered in a seductive voice, "I'm fine now." Wil swallowed hard trying to stop himself from blushing. She stood there for a moment longer, their eyes locked. Finally, she stepped away from him. "Your turn, Jess," she said.

For the next week, every day, Wil had looked forward to seeing Rochelle. Every day had started with a joke, her laughter was intoxicating to him. Three weeks later and out of the four women that had started the gym only Rochelle was left. She would come in, make a beeline straight for Wil. "Shall we box today?" she had said as soon as they met.

Wil had smiled, "So, you think you can take me?" he said.

"Put your gloves on and let's find out, big boy," she said with confidence.

Wil stood in the ring with Rochelle. The buzzer sounded, she jumped forward throwing a straight left. Wil blocked this with ease and continued to circle her. Rochelle threw another left, then a right, then a left, each one Wil blocked. "Are you going to hit back?" she had asked.

"I will," he said, lightly throwing a right jab that caught her on the forehead.

From behind old Jack shouted out, "Careful there Wil, she looks like a killer this one." His concentration broken he had turned to look, when he turned back around Rochelle's glove hit him square on the nose. Blood started to flow and the look of shock on Rochelle's face was priceless.

"Are you okay?" she asked him.

"I'm fine don't worry," he said.

"I'm really sorry. I thought you would have blocked it."

"Rochelle, I'm fine," he assured her.

She started to laugh. "I'm so sorry," she repeated.

Wil looked at her. "Can I ask you something?"

"Yes, of course," she replied, still laughing.

"Well, I've been wanting to ask you if, err, you'd maybe want to go for a drink or something?" She had looked at him with a raised eyebrow. "If not, I understand," he added quickly.

"I'd love to!" she said. Wil's heart had soared in that moment. That night they had met, Wil had been standing outside the bar waiting for her. He was wearing jeans and a white short sleeved shirt, the shirt showing off the size of his biceps and hugging to his chest. The door to the bar opened and a group of women came out, one of them tried to engage Wil in conversation. She was a little drunk and kept placing her hands on his arm. Then he saw her walking towards him, Rochelle was wearing a black sequined dress that came halfway down her thighs and hugged to her body showing off her curves. The sequins shone as she walked towards him, this only highlighted her light brown skin. Her long black hair hung down past her shoulders. Wil could no longer hear the other woman, only the beating of his heart as Rochelle walked towards him. Other men stopped and turned to look at her, the other girl still talking to Wil hadn't even noticed. He wasn't paying any attention to her; his eyes were fixed directly on Rochelle. Wil could feel his heart quicken as this vision of beauty walked towards him. Wil stepped past the other girl who seemed shocked. She was even more shocked when Rochelle walked up to him, placed both arms around his neck and pulled him in to a kiss.

The other girl walked away looking back at Rochelle. "Bitch!" shouted the woman. Wil, still stunned from the kiss, looked at Rochelle.

"Wow, what was that for?" he asked.

Taking his hand and leading him into the bar Rochelle answered, "That's to show everyone that you're with me."

The night had been great, Rochelle had talked about her life, Wil had felt comfortable talking with her — his uncomfortableness around women had disappeared with Rochelle. As the night drew to an end, Wil hailed a taxi. "What's your address?" he asked her.

She smiled at him. "Silly boy, I'm coming home with you," she told him. The night of passion was one that Wil would never forget. They had made love for over an hour, both climaxing several times. Then they had both fallen asleep in each other's arms. Shouting came from downstairs which broke his day dream.

Vanessa was shouting. "Look," Wil heard her say. "You know how important this trip is to me and Wil just be here on time. I don't care if you bring along a mate, that's fine. Just make sure they behave. I don't want any arguments. Okay John, look, just be here in the morning. Christ." Wil looked down at the sleeping form of Rochelle, pulled back the bed covers and slipped in beside her. She stirred turning and put her arm across his chest.

Kissing her forehead he whispered, "I love you."

Sleepily she mumbled back, "And I love you." Wil heard the fridge door bang shut and Vanessa curse. Better to leave her alone, his sister had a temper when she'd had a drink. He flicked the lamp off and sleep came quickly.

Downstairs Vanessa had just opened another bottle of wine. John could be a pain in the arse at the best of times but their relationship was one of understanding. He never complained about her being away for months at a time, but the last time they had argued Wil had stepped in and a fight had started... Well, if you could call it a fight. John had thrown a clumsy punch that Wil had easily blocked. Two of John's friends had stepped in, one jumping to Wil's back while the other had run straight at him. Wil had flipped the guy from his back cannoning him into the oncoming attacker. Both hit the floor hard. They both got back to their feet looking groggy. John had rushed in at Wil with another clumsy attack. Wil had just side stepped and a little push to John's back had sent him face first into the wall. Vanessa had screamed at them all to stop. Wil held up his hands. "I haven't thrown a single punch yet," he told her.

John was slowly getting back to his feet when one of his friends pushed Vanessa out of the way. "Stay out of this bitch!" he said. Looking at Wil he added, "Now you fucker, I'm going to smash your bastard face in."

Vanessa saw the change in her brother's face and knew that Wil was now serious. The first attacker had run in and went down from a hard right cross. The man fell down like he'd been poleaxed and laid there not moving. Wil now looked at the second attacker who had now grabbed a beer bottle from the table. He had run, swinging the bottle at Wil's head which he parried, grabbing a hold of the man's arm. Wil spun the man which sent him crashing into John who was just getting back to his feet. The man with the bottle turned and screamed, running at Wil, again he ducked under another wild swing that carried the man past him. As the man turned again Wil delivered a huge uppercut to the man's chin which lifted him from the floor to land on the table. He rolled off, hit the floor and didn't move. Wil had not seen John come up behind him, he just felt a hand grab him and pull him around. The punch hit Wil flush on the jaw. It lacked any power. Wil hit John with a vicious head butt causing him to stagger back. As his vision cleared John saw the punch that would render him unconscious. The bouncers had come running into the beer garden and Vanessa had stood in front of her brother. "Don't fight back, just leave," she said. "I'll talk with them."

"I tried not to hurt them," he told her. "But I can only take so much of his shit. You could do better, sis." Without another word, Wil had turned and left. Vanessa drained the glass of wine.

"Please let John behave himself," she said aloud. Walking to the kitchen she placed the glass in the dishwasher and headed for bed.

Chapter 2

Wil stepped from the shower, wrapping the towel around his waist and made his way to the bedroom where Rochelle was still sleeping.

"Babe, wake up. Come on. We have a long drive ahead of us and we need to get there before it gets dark."

Moaning Rochelle turned over. "What time is it?" she asked.

"Five thirty a.m.," Wil replied.

Rochelle looked at him. "Are you kidding? Come back to bed."

"We can't," Wil told her. "We have to get ready. John will be here soon and it's a five-and-a-half-hour drive."

Kneeling up on the bed, she grabbed hold of the t-shirt she was wearing and slipped it clear, revealing her naked body.

"Are you sure you can't spare thirty minutes for me?" With a huge grin on his face Wil removed the towel, throwing it at her and dived on the bed. Rochelle squealed with delight as Wil took hold of her.

A knock came from the door followed by Vanessa's voice. "We don't have time for that you two! Come on, you need to get ready."

"Sorry, sis," answered Wil. "We'll be right down."

"If you think I'm loading the mini bus by myself

you're mistaken," she added. "What's the point in all those muscles you have if you let your sister do all the work."

"Sorry," shouted Rochelle. "We're getting up now." They both heard Vanessa walk away. Rochelle looked at Wil and said, "Well get a move on before she comes back, we'll have to make this one a quickie!"

The doorbell rang and Vanessa made her way to the door, opening it. There stood John, with a bunch of flowers. "For you my sweet lady." He gave an elaborate bow. John was a man in his twenties, average build, black-curly hair and blue eyed.

Smiling, Vanessa accepted them, inhaling the sweet aroma. Then looking at John asked, "What have you done?"

"Nothing," he said with a pained expression on his face. "I'm on time, the mini bus is filled with fuel, I have the supplies you told me to get, I haven't seen you in two months, so I thought what better way than to say hello to a beautiful lady than with a beautiful bunch of flowers that pale at the side of her beauty."

"That's so corny, John," said Vanessa. "But I'll accept the compliment. Can you start and load the bags in? Wil should be down shortly he and Rochelle are just finishing packing."

John turned round and whistled towards the minibus. The door opened and out stepped a young man with blond hair, tall and slim. "Vanessa this is my good buddy, Dave. He'll be coming with us."

Vanessa held out her hand. "Nice to meet you, Dave."

"Likewise," he answered. "John is a lucky man, wow! You're even prettier than he said!"

"Hey," interrupted John. "That's my girlfriend when you're done."

Vanessa patted his cheek. "Put the bags in the van, I'll go and get Wil." With that she turned and walked back into the house.

Wil's voice shouted out, "Nessy, have you packed my bow?"

"Yes, it's out here with the other bags," she called back. "And if you call me Nessy again I'll shoot you with it. Get a move on, we need to be going."

Dave looked at John. "Did he just say bow? Does he mean bow like bow and arrows?"

"Yep," answered John.

"Wait a minute," said Dave. "Just who is this guy? Does he think he's fucking Rambo?" he said smiling.

John laughed. "No. Vanessa's dad used to take her and her brother on survival trips to this cabin in Scotland, teaching them to live off the land, hunt down their own food, all kinds of survival crap. Wil's kind of a bad ass, he knows boxing, Karate, MMA and some other shit I have no idea how to pronounce. I think their dad is in the SAS," said John.

"For real, man, this guy can do all that, and you're fucking his sister and cheating on her when she's away on her business trips. Dude, I'd hate to be you. If he finds out he'll fucking kill you."

John laughed. "He doesn't scare me. I could kick his ass if I wanted to."

Dave looked over John's shoulder. "Hey man, you

must be Wil," he said.

John spun round with a look of panic on his face but no one was there. "You fucking prick, Smithy," said John, using Dave's nick name.

Dave's laughter peeled out. "I thought you said you could kick his ass."

"Just fuck off, Smithy," replied John. "And put those bags in the van."

A car pulled up behind the minibus and three people got out and headed towards the house. "Who are those two losers?" asked Dave. "And that is one fine looking girl," he added.

"That would be Tom, Wil's best friend, and his girlfriend, Mary. The small fat one is Brad, he hangs round Wil and Vanessa like a fly round shit. I think he has a crush on Nessa."

Dave gave a low whistle. "Damn, I'd like to have a night with that Mary, she's a fox. Look at those hips, swish."

John grabbed a bag and tossed it to his friend. "Come on, let's get this finished."

Mary heard the whistle, she turned and smiled at the two men. She was a pretty young girl, eighteen years old with a pretty smile, long blonde hair, blue eyes and loved the attention that her smile got her from men. Even more she loved the reaction from Tom when other men paid attention to her, and loved that after a year together he still got jealous.

The three of them continued towards the house. Brad kept looking back at the two men loading the bags into the minibus. As he turned round, he bumped into Wil who was standing in the driveway holding a huge bag with Rochelle at his side. "Whoa there, Brad, I know you need glasses but how can you miss me?"

Wil took a step back to look at what Brad was wearing. Brad had dressed himself in a beige shirt and shorts along with desert boots. "I like your choice of cloths for the trip," commented Wil. "But you could have just worn sports gear like the rest of us. You kind of look like Ray Mears if he wore glasses and had ginger hair."

Tom started to laugh. "He's too busy being nosey, aren't you Bradley?" said Tom.

"Why is John here?" asked Brad. "And who's that with him?"

"Relax," Wil told him. "John's here for Nessy and that's just his friend from work. Nessy says he's okay."

"I don't like him," added Brad. "And Vanessa hates it when you call her Nessy."

Wil put his arm around Brad's shoulder. "Relax my friend. I'll handle John if he starts. I'll kick his arse again."

Brad gave a sigh. "Okay but what does Vanessa see in him? He's a complete dickhead, I hate him so much."

Tom patted Brad on the back. "You only hate him because you've been in love with Vanessa since you were ten years old."

"Oh, that's so sweet," said Rochelle. "Is that true?"

Turning, Brad tried to slap Tom who ducked under the slap. "Why would you tell everyone that?" he asked. "Why do you have to embarrass me every chance you get?"

Mary stepped in and hugged him. "It's okay, Brad.

37

We all know how you feel about Vanessa. I think its sweet that you love her like you do." She then looked at Tom. "And if you don't stop teasing him you will be in the tent on your own on this trip!"

Tom's eyes narrowed and he looked at his friend who was still in Mary's arms. "Sorry bro," he said. "I'll lay off the jokes."

Wil interrupted them all, "Come on now guys, let's just chill and enjoy this trip."

Vanessa came walking from the house with the last of the bags. Seeing Brad, Tom and Mary, gave them all a kiss on the cheek. Brad got a hug from her which made him redden and smile. "Okay guys. Are we all ready for this trip?" asked Vanessa. "Wil, did you call Angus to make sure everything is okay?"

"I did," answered Wil. "But only got the answerphone. We can call him from the road while we're travelling."

John and Dave came over. "That's all the bags loaded. Let's get moving, shall we?" said John. Dave took hold of John's arm as the other walked to get in the minibus.

"Who's this Angus?" he asked.

"Some army buddy of Vanessa's dad, I think," answered John.

"Well just letting you know I have the you know what in my pocket," he said, producing a small plastic bag with white powder in it.

"Put that away!" snapped John. "If Vanessa sees it she'll go crazy. Just get in the damn van. Christ, you're so dumb sometimes."

The creature had tracked its prey where it had barricaded itself in. It had advanced slowly towards its victim when it had emerged carrying a small black object. The creature had stopped and studied the small man in front of it. Then there had been a deafening sound coming from the black object, that had caused pain in the creature's shoulder. It had turned and fled.

The next day the creature had returned. Again, the man had come to meet it carrying the black object, this time the creature kept its distance. The man lowered the object, the creature took a couple of steps forward and the man raised it again. The creature stopped and retreated a few steps, the man lowered the black object. For a moment the creature studied the man then turned and loped off.

Angus lowered the gun and went back inside the cabin. Morag was laid on the couch, her skin pale, she had a fever. As he approached her, she opened her eyes. "Is it still out there?" she asked.

"Aye, lass, it is," answered Angus. "Smart bastard too. It knows the range of the gun and won't come within firing range. I hit it once but the damage wasn't much. I don't know how much longer we can hold out here."

"I just need a few days," she told him. "Then we can make a run for it." Angus stroked her hair back from her face and she fell asleep again. Returning to the window, he looked out at the quad, it had taken damage in the first attack. The fuel line had been severed, the quad was useless. Even if he repaired it, they had no fuel for it. Morag's condition was getting worse and he was running out of time and ideas.

The creature returned to the cave that it and its mate had set up as a lair. The bones of the animals they had feasted upon lay all over the floor. The two creatures were now having to roam further to find food. The few wild sheep had all but been slain and the rabbits hardly made a meal. The deer were harder to catch as they were swifter than the lumbering sheep, yet still nothing tasted as nice as the blood from the man creature with the loud weapon. As the wounded creature settled down to rest, the larger of the two headed out to hunt. It ran for a few miles at an easy lope then came to a stop. A new scent filled its nostrils. Turning its huge head, taking in deep shuddering breaths, its body started to quiver, saliva dripping from its mouth. At speed it set off in the direction of the possible meal. The light was starting to fade as the creature came upon the camp site. Two tents were set out in a clearing, loud noises that hurt its ears were coming from a small metal box. It was wary to approach and settled down in the undergrowth and watched. A figure emerged from the closest tent. The scent of the man made the beast's mouth water as it anticipated the fresh meat. Then a second figure appeared, the creature bunched its muscles ready to attack.

Steve looked over at the light coming from the other tent before turning to Amanda. "Turn the music down please," he asked her.

"Yo, Kev. Are you and Dianne joining us for something to eat?"

"In a minute," Steve answered Kev. "We're just finishing our evening exercise," he shouted.

Laughter came from the tent followed by a woman's voice. "Don't say that! Those two are unbelievable!" said Amanda. "They have sex at every possible opportunity."

"Okay for some," answered Steve.

Amanda screwed her face up at him. "You'll get yours later," she added, smiling.

Steve knelt down and stirred the pot of soup that had just started to bubble. Kev and Dianne came out of the tent and joined the others. "So, what's for dinner?" asked Kev.

"Soup," came the reply from the other three people. "Fresh off the gas stove."

"You know a man could quickly go off soup," he added. "I'd love a nice juicy steak or some chicken right now."

A low rumbling sound came from behind Kev. Steve looked over at his friend. "You're not kidding? Was that your stomach?"

"No," answered Kev with a bemused look on his face. "That wasn't me."

The bushes nearby exploded as a beast of nightmare came crashing out and into the camp. The four companions had no time to react, the beast was upon them. A huge mouth closed around the head of the nearest person. Kev was thrown into the air, with a slash of its paw it disembowelled the next person. Steve's body slumped to the floor. The two women were up and running, screaming as they fled. The creature gave chase. It slashed out with its huge paw, opening a wound in the closest person's leg as they ran. Dianne tripped and rolled as pain ran through her leg. She managed to get back to her feet, pain lanced through her back. Dianne's body was almost torn in half from the slashing blow. The creature stood and looked around, it had lost the fourth person and could only smell the blood that filled the air. From under its chest, near the armpits, came two small arms which gathered up the body.

It stood sniffing the air then returned to the camp. It sat and ate, discarding the entrails. The flesh was exquisite, the marrow rich as it crunched through the bones. Eating its fill, the creature looked round the campsite, the smell of burning wafted to its nostrils. It stood and sniffed at the boiling soup. It snorted and with a flick of its paw it sent the gas stove tumbling towards the tents. Instantly the tent caught fire — bright light bathed the campsite. Pain flared through its leg as the flames touched its skin. The creature let out a terrible howl, gathering the other bodies, it fled from the campsite and headed back to the cave and its mate.

A short distance away, hidden behind a large rock sat Amanda, frozen in fear. Every fibre of her body telling her to run, but her legs wouldn't obey her. Then the howl had come and she had started to cry, holding her hands over her mouth. For what seemed an eternity she had sat there shivering. At last, she forced herself to her feet and slowly made her way back to the campsite. She passed the pool of blood that had come from Dianne's body but that was nothing compared to the horror that greeted her as she walked into camp. The tents had burnt away and now were smouldering, entrails of someone laid on the floor.

Amanda gagged and then vomited. She looked

around but the bodies had gone. The footprints left by whatever had attacked them were huge and three toed. Quickly she searched through what was left of the camp, gathered some supplies and set off in the opposite direction, constantly looking back. The moon was full which bathed the hills in a silver light. She had run for what seemed an eternity — her legs ached but fear kept her going. In the distance she could see what looked like a large wooded area. Stopping to catch her breath she squatted down. Movement from her right caused her to scream out. The sheep ran from her. "You have to get a grip woman," she said out loud.

Setting off again, this time to the woods and the sanctuary of the trees. "At least in there I can hide till morning," she said to herself. Thoughts of her friends brought tears to her eyes as she ran on. Her friends were all dead, that thing had come from nowhere, its skin as black as night. The noise as it bit the head off Kevin, the howl had made her blood run cold. What did she know about camping out in the wild? She had left all this to Steve. With a deep breath and a shake of her head she continued towards the woods.

John yawned. "I need to take a break," he said aloud. "We'll stop at the next service station."

"Great!" answered Dave. "I need to piss like a race horse." No one laughed. "Wow, tough crowd," said Dave. "Come on guys, lighten up. Let's have some stories or some jokes told. We're supposed to be having fun but all you guys have done is sleep for the past few hours."

Vanessa looked over at Dave. "You seem very hyper.

Are you okay?"

"I'm fine love, how about you?" John looked back at his friend from the rear-view mirror and raised an eyebrow giving his friend a warning look.

Dave turned, looking at Mary. "So, how long have you two been together?" he asked her.

Tom leant forward. "What has that to do with you?" he asked, more sternly than he had meant to.

Mary had put a hand on his shoulder. "Tom, no need to be like that," she said. "We've been together just over a year now," she told him.

Dave smiled. "That's nice. Has he proposed yet? A beautiful girl like you needs to be kept happy."

Tom lent forward again. "Dude, I do keep my girl happy and again, what has it to do with you?"

"Whoa, whoa, man chill out! I was just complimenting you on your girlfriend. You must be doing something right to keep her for a year. Just relax man and take the compliment, I'm only trying to get to know you guys."

"Well," said Tom defensively. "Now you know how long we've been together just don't get too familiar with my girlfriend."

Dave held his hands up in surrender and moved to the next seat where Brad was sat reading a book. Mary looked at Tom. "That was a bit harsh," she told him.

"I don't like the way he looks at you," he said. "There's something funny about that guy."

Brad looked up from his book to see the smiling face of Dave. "Hi there," said Dave with a friendly smile. "What's the book about?"

Brad looked at the man. "It's about the JFK assassination and the theory that it was the US government who ordered his death."

"I don't know who JFK is." Brad looked at the man in disbelief.

"You don't know who JF—"

Dave interrupted him. "So, what's your name? How do you know Wil and Vanessa? Have you got a girlfriend? If yes, why hasn't she come along on the trip?"

Brad seemed shocked at the verbosity of questions thrown at him. "I'm currently single," he stammered. "And my name is Bradley, but most call me Brad."

"Well Brad, I'm Dave, but you can call me Smithy. And since I'm a fifth wheel we'll stick together on this trip. What do you think?" Brad just stared back in disbelief.

Smithy turned, looked at the others on the mini bus. Wil sat with his head resting on the window, his eyes shut. Rochelle leaning against him idly, scrolling on her mobile phone. She looked up seeing Dave smiling at her. She returned his smile, then the questions started.

"So, Rochelle," he asked. "How long have you and the man mountain been together? How did you two meet?"

Sitting forward, Rochelle put her phone down. "Well, we've been together a couple of months now, we met at the gym. I started there making a complete fool of myself, Wil came over and showed me where my technique was wrong. I took one look into those big brown eyes of his and I went weak at the knee."

45

"Did he ask you out straight away?" interrupted Smithy. "I would have, you're gorgeous."

Rochelle shook her head. "No, he didn't and thank you for the compliment. It took him a couple of weeks to ask me out. To tell you the truth I was about to ask him. I'd done my very best to flirt with him wearing tight yoga pants, bending over every time he looked over at me, squeezing his arms, brushing up against him. I even laughed at his bad jokes. I've never had to flirt so hard in my life!"

Vanessa turned round in the front seat. "That's my brother for you, clueless when it comes to the opposite sex."

With his eyes still shut Wil spoke. "I can hear you!"

Rochelle turned and kissed him. "Aaawwww baby, I take it back, your jokes are funny," she said, her laughter peeling out. The others' laughter filled the minibus.

Wil pulled Rochelle into him and hugged her tight. "So, John tells me your dad is in the army," said Dave.

"Was," said Wil.

"Oh, what does he do now?" inquired Dave.

"He's dead," answered Wil, his face and mood darkening at the question.

Vanessa snapped at her brother. "Don't say it like that Wil! The man was only asking."

"Sorry, Dave," said Wil.

Vanessa continued, "Our dad died just over a year ago from a brain aneurysm. It hit us both extremely hard, we were raised by our father. We lost our mother at a young age, she was killed in a car crash, the other driver was drunk. Wil and I don't really remember her, so we were both raised as army brats."

"Whoa I'm sorry," said Dave. "I had no idea. A heads up would have been nice, John."

"Sorry," came the reply from John. "Completely forgot to mention it to you."

"That's because you're a dick," muttered Brad under his breath.

"Sorry, what was that?" asked John.

"I said how long to the service station. I need to pee," Brad answered sheepishly.

"Not long now," said John.

"So, Wil?" asked Dave. "What's the bow for?"

"It's just for a bit of hunting. If I can't snare any rabbits, I may be able to bring down a couple of pheasants, so we have some fresh meat."

"This may be a stupid question," said Dave. "But there's nothing up there that could attack us, right?"

John's laughter boomed out. "Smithy you dumb shit, we're going to Scotland not fucking Africa. What are you expecting? Prides of lions roaming round?"

Everyone started to laugh. "Screw you John, I was only asking."

Through his laughter, Bard managed to say, "There are no large predatory animals in Scotland, Dave. We'll be quite safe."

"And there's Professor Brad with another interesting fact," said Tom.

Mary tapped Tom on the back of his head. "Be nice," she told him. "Or you won't be getting any alone time with me."

"Its fine up there Dave. The biggest thing we'll see

47

will be a deer if we're lucky or a couple of sheep that have strayed away from their flock," said Wil. "The bow is for small game only and we have a loch nearby we can do some fishing in if you guys want to?"

"I've never fished before," said Dave.

"That's okay, I'll teach you," said Vanessa. "It's quite relaxing."

Mary leaned forward. "John, turn the radio up, please, I love this song."

John did as he was asked and the bus was filled with the sound of the three girls singing along to the lyrics while looking at their partners. Brad sat there looking uncomfortable, then he saw the sign, "services one mile ahead". As the minibus came to a stop everyone started to exit. John called for Dave to stay behind. When all the others were out of earshot John looked at his friend. "Are you fucking crazy? How much coke have you had?" he asked.

"Only a little," Dave answered. "Look have some yourself, it will keep you awake and stop you being so fucking boring." Dave took the small bag of coke out of his pocket and John dipped the key in, sniffing the drug up his nostril. "Just try and keep calm, Ness is looking at you suspiciously. I thought you were going to end it with her anyway?" his friend asked. "Who's that other girl you've been sticking your dick in?"

John smiled. "Jamie," he said. "Now, that girl does love a good time. Look I'm going to have this free trip away with Ness then cut her loose. I tried to be faithful but when she's away my balls end up like water melons. I'm sick of relieving myself," he said jerking his hand up and down.

Dave laughed, and put his arm around his friend's shoulder. "Can I have a crack at Vanessa?" he said laughing.

John gave a chuckle. "Be my guest," he said.

Chapter three

Wil sat down in the restaurant to a huge plate of steak, chips and veg. Rochelle sat at the side of him with a salad sandwich. She kept leaning over and stealing a chip from Wil's plate. Every time she did this, he glared at her, to which she returned the glare with an innocent smile. "If you want some chips, why didn't you order some?" he asked her.

"I can't eat a full portion," she told him.

"But you've eaten half of mine!" he said.

She smiled again, this time stealing the piece of steak off his fork and quickly putting it in her mouth. She kissed him, stood up and asked Mary and Vanessa if they needed to use the bathroom. The other two girls stood and walked off with Rochelle. She turned round and blew a kiss at Wil.

"Why do woman all go to the toilet at the same time?" Tom asked. The others just looked and shrugged.

"Don't know," said Wil. "Don't really care. What I do know is I need something else now to fill me since she's nicked half of my food. I wonder if they have any apple pie." He stood and walked off in search of dessert.

Tom shook his head looking at Brad. "Have you ever seen anyone eat as much as Wil? Where does he put it all?"

Brad pushed his glasses back up his nose with his finger. "You know that Wil's calorie intake is probably double of yours. He needs that amount to keep his body in tip top form."

"Oh my god, Brad. Could you just say 'yeah dude I know what you mean, his legs must be hollow or something'? Why the textbook answer, all the time?"

Brad looked at his friend confused. "It's a true fact though and why would Wil's legs be hollow?"

Tom laughed at his answer. "Dude you need to learn to chill, not everything can be learnt from a book."

Tom looked around. "Where are John and Dave? They didn't follow us in from the minibus."

Brad looked round. "I'll go and see where they are. We need to stick to Wil's travel schedule." He stood up from the table and headed off without another word. He passed Wil who was heading back to the table with a large slab of apple pie and whipped cream.

"Just checking the travel schedule," he told his friend and carried on walking. Wil took his seat at the table, smiled at Tom and spooned in a large piece of the pie. With a huge satisfying grin, he started to chew the food. Tom smiled back and pointed behind him. Wil raised an eyebrow in question. The slender hand of Rochelle came over his shoulder and scooped some of the whipped cream off his plate. Before he could say anything, she had slid onto his lap taken the spoon from his hand and started to eat the pie.

Brad could see the minibus at the fuel pump and walked over. The two friends were deep in conversation and didn't notice his approach.

"So," said John. "This one time I was with Jamie, we were out drinking and her friend was super drunk and I knew that this was my chance for a three way. Jamie was game from the start. We got back to my place and the fun started. We were right in the middle of it all and my phone rings and guess who's on the phone."

"Who?" asked Dave barley able to keep the excitement from his voice.

"It was only Vanessa ringing me while I'm doing these two girls."

"No way!" exclaimed Dave. "What did you do?"

"I sat back and had the call with Vanessa while the two girls carried on, while I watched. As soon as I had told Vanessa I missed her and loved her she hung up and I joined back in the threesome."

Brad dropped his book. John turned quickly, a look of shock on his face. "How long have you been stood there?" he asked.

"Only a couple of seconds," replied Brad. "I just wanted to make sure we're sticking to Wil's schedule," he stammered.

John looked at him. "Go and tell the others we're ready to go." Brad picked up his book and hurried away. John looked at his friend. "Do you think he heard us?"

"No idea bro, but if he did, you're screwed."

John looked at Brad as he hurried away. "I hate that fat bastard! Have you seen the way he looks at Ness? I'm sure he fancies her."

"What do you care?" asked Dave. "You're banging another girl and ending it with Ness anyway."

"That's not the point!" snapped John. "Could you

imagine if I lost a girl as pretty as Ness to that fat twat?"

"I'd be more worried about that huge fucker of a brother of hers ripping you to pieces," said Dave smiling and slapping his friend on the shoulder. Well, we'll soon find out if she knows, here they come," he added pointing over his friends' shoulder. "She doesn't look angry and Wil has Rochelle in a piggy back carry... Unless she's trying to choke him out before he gets to you."

John turned. "Funny fucker, aren't you?" he said sarcastically.

Vanessa walked past him and kissed his cheek. "Are you still okay to drive, or should I?"

"I'm okay babe," he said. "Thanks for the offer, let's get moving." John looked over at Dave who gave him a thumbs up and then disappeared into the minibus.

Within ten minutes Wil was asleep, his head on the window and the dreams came again of his father. He was stood in the kitchen, tears streaming down his face. The five-year-old boy heart-broken, his father wiping the blood from his nose.

"Tell me what happened."

Wil tried but the tears started and he couldn't speak. His father looked at his sister. "Okay Ness, tell me what's gone off."

"The older boys had taken my dolly, daddy," she began. "And were calling me Loch Ness monster. Wil told them to stop and they pushed him over, but he got back up and one of the older boys hit Wil in the nose. Wil hit him back, daddy, but then two other boys pushed Wil over and they all hit him. I hit one in the face with my dolly. He said, if I was a boy, he would punch me so I kicked him in his leg then the other boy pushed me over."

"Okay," said Alex. "What are their names?"

"The boy that hit Wil was Jack Cartwright. The one who had my dolly was Ronny Philips. I don't know who the other one was," she told her father.

Alex held up his hand for Vanessa to be quiet then looked at them both. "I'm proud of you both for sticking up for each other but aren't those boys nine years old."

Wil looked at his father and nodded his head. His right eye had swollen shut and his bottom lip had a split in it. "You need to be able to know when to fight back son," he had told him. "I know that you are bigger than most of the boys in your class but you were outnumbered and they were stronger than you. I'll go talk with their fathers, you two go and get in the bath and get ready for bed."

A week had gone by and Wil's eye was nearly back to normal. The twins were playing in the garden when they heard their father's voice calling them from the garage. Instantly, they were up and running, as they entered the garage, they both stopped at the door, their father had completely changed the garage. Gone were the tools and lawn mower and the old dusty boxes, in their place now hung a punch bag and a treadmill was also on the back wall with other kinds of exercise equipment that the twins had never seen.

Alex looked at his children. "Okay," he said. "Now you two are going to learn how to fight and how to defend yourselves. You must only do what I teach you both in here. If you are threatened, you must never use this to bully other children. Is that understood?"

The twins looked at each other and nodded in agreement. For weeks Alex pushed his children to the point of exhaustion. At first, they had complained but Alex ignored this. Every day his children were made to exercise for two hours, then they could play. The summer holidays came and Alex increased the exercise to three hours per day. Vanessa hated it but Wil seemed to love it more and more. At five years old Wil was a big child already he was the size of the average eight-to-nine-year-old. This made him a target for the older boys. The summer holidays came and went and the years rolled on. Wil and Vanessa did what their father told them and by the time Wil was eleven he stood at five feet nine inches tall, his body starting to show the man he would become. Vanessa was of average height for her age but the years of training had made her wolf lean while Wil was bulking up.

The twins had started high school and on the first day their father had seen his children off to school. The day had started well until Wil was tripped in the corridor. He looked up to see Jack and Ronny laughing at him. Wil felt a hand on his arm as a teacher helped him to his feet. "Thank you, Mr Dunn," said Wil.

"You're welcome lad, try and be more careful," he said. "You could hurt yourself."

"I will, sir," replied Wil.

At lunchtime, Vanessa found her brother sitting quietly at the edge of the sports field eating his dinner. She sat beside him. "How's the day going?" she asked.

Wil shrugged his shoulders. "You know," came his reply. Just then something hit Wil on the back of the head, followed by laughter. Wil and Vanessa turned to see Jack and Ronny stood there. Wil looked down, one of them had thrown an orange at him which had hit him on the back of his head.

"Oops," said Jack. "Sorry about that."

Vanessa stood up. "Just leave us alone!" she snapped.

"Wow, everyone look, the Loch Ness monster can talk," said Jack. The others gathered around and started to laugh.

Wil got to his feet. "Don't call my sister that!" he said in a deep voice, his anger threatening to overwhelm him.

"Or what?" said Ronny, throwing another orange that hit Vanessa in the chest.

Ronny never saw it coming. Wil had run forward, jumping through the air his knee cannoning under Ronny's chin. He hit the floor and didn't move. Jack stood for a moment, open mouthed, looking at his friend. Then he turned, throwing a punch at Wil's face which was blocked with ease. Stepping forward, Wil delivered a savage head-butt that broke Jack's nose. Everyone heard the bone break. Jack staggered back holding his hands to his face. "You bastard!" he shouted. "You broke my fucking nose!"

Wil just stood there, hands raised in defence. Jack ran forward, Wil sidestepped tripping him to the floor. The other children round them started laughing at Jack. Jeers of "Jack's getting his ass kicked by a first year" started. Jack got back to his feet and this time slowly came forward. He threw a right cross at Wil which was blocked. Wil followed this with a straight left jab followed by a right cross that spun Jack from his feet. He landed face first on the floor, pushing his arms underneath him he managed to get to his knees. His vision blurred. As he blinked to clear his vision, he saw Vanessa stood in front of him.

"If you were a man," she said. Then with a right cross, hit him full in the face. Jack slumped to the floor and didn't move.

Wil and Vanessa were sat in the headmaster's office when their father walked in. He looked at his children and smiled. "Mr Dunn," said Alex, extending his hand. "What's happened?"

Mr Dunn shook the outstretched hand. "Please, take a seat." Mr Dunn started to explain about the fight. "So Mr Jameson, I'm sure you can understand that we don't tolerate this kind of behaviour in school."

"I'm glad to hear this," said Alex. "I hope that you will be taking the full action against the two fifth year students that attacked my children. I'm sure that the board of governors wouldn't like to hear of such things. It's a good job my son and daughter know self-defence, otherwise they could have been hurt. I'll take them home and make sure that they are both okay."

Mr Dunn had sat there with his mouth wide open. "Come on you two," said Alex. "Let's be off, I need to get you home." Without another word he left the office and his children followed.

In the car on the way home, both Vanessa and Wil sat quiet. Alex looked in the rear-view mirror at his two children. "Okay," he said. "Talk me through what happened."

Wil took a deep breath. "This morning I was walking

to my lesson when one of them tripped me in the corridor. I didn't react, Mr Dunn was there and helped me up and sent everyone on their way. At lunch time I found a nice quiet spot and started to eat."

"That's when I joined him, dad," interrupted Vanessa.

"We were just minding our own business when one of them threw an orange at Wil's head. Then they started with the name calling again."

"Jack threw another orange, hitting Ness in the chest," added Wil. "So, I reacted."

"How did you react?" asked his father, his eyebrow raised.

"Well, I was out numbered two to one. I knew I had to even the odds, removing one of my opponents so I then could take out the other. Ronny was laughing at Ness and not watching me so I ran in with a flying knee to the chin, rendering him unconscious. Then I knew that Jack would attack. I countered his attack which was easy, when he was beaten, I backed away. Ness threw the final punch knocking him out."

Alex was watching Vanessa's face as she tried to hide the smile forming on her lips. "Good," answered Alex. "So, you reacted to protect your sister and you didn't start the trouble in the first place. I think those two will have learned their lesson now but be wary around them, they may yet seek revenge for the embarrassment."

Their father was right. Twice more Jack tried to get revenge on Wil and failed both times. Each one saw Jack unconscious. As for Ronny, he never bothered Wil again, or Vanessa for that matter.

Life seemed to go smoother for the twins from then on.

The minibus hit a pothole in the road causing Wil to wake from his dream. Looking round he knew where they were and it was only around an hour now before they would arrive at the farm. He felt the excitement grow in his body. It had been his father's funeral the last time he had seen Angus and revelled in the stories of how Angus and his father had served together in the forces. He loved the old man and his wife Morag. They were family to him and Vanessa but since the death of his father, Wil had constantly talked with Angus on the phone, he was now the closest thing Wil had to a father. An hour later the minibus pulled up in the farmyard, the friends exited the minibus, stretching, tired and stiff limbed.

Vanessa looked at her watch. Two p.m., which still gave them a few hours of daylight. Wil had moved straight for the front door of the house, knocking first then trying the door. It was locked. He stepped back.

"Angus, Morag, are you here?" he shouted. Turning and looking at his sister he shrugged his shoulders. He walked back over to where the others were stood.

"Is there a problem?" asked Tom, seeing the look on his friend's face.

"I don't know," answered Wil. "They knew we were coming, it's strange they aren't here to meet us. I'll go check round the back of the farm, they may be down in the fields."

Wil set of at a run, disappearing round the side of the farmhouse. Vanessa looked at the others. "Well come on, get the stuff out of the bus."

The others did as they were bid. Within a few minutes Wil was back. "Nothing," he said. "No one about, no animals are in the pens or the field. Somethings not right," he told his sister.

She put a calming hand on his shoulder. "Look, the Land Rover is over there, they can't have gone far."

He took a deep breath. "The quad isn't in the barn, maybe he's gone to the cabin?"

"Stop worrying," she told her brother. "We'll find them and I'm sure there's a perfectly good explanation for what's going on, you'll see."

Wil nodded, then smiled. "Okay guys, come on. Let's get moving, I want to be at the first camp site before it gets dark."

Rochelle walked to her boyfriend with a nervous look on her face. "You okay babe? You look nervous."

"I'm fine," she answered. "So long as you're with me. I'll look after you next half-term. How about that beach holiday and you can show me that bikini?"

Rochelle gave a warm smile, kissed him and gave a cheeky wink. "Deal," she said.

Tom came over and interrupted their moment of passion. "Err, Wil, can I have a word?" Rochelle moved off to the other girls. "I thought you said we were going to a cabin, yet we have tents. So are we camping or going to this cabin?"

"Dude," answered Wil. "I could get you to the cabin in around five hours if we walked straight for it but we're going to a couple of campsites first, live off the land, bathe in cool lochs, swim, fish and enjoy nature."

Tom leaned in to his friend. "I'm all for the camping

shit bro but the only thing I'm bothered about is getting Mary alone and you know…"

Wil stood looking at his friend. "So, what's stopping you?" he asked. "You'll be able to 'you know' all you like."

Tom blushed a little. "It's going to be hard with you guys camped round us."

Wil raised an eyebrow. "Please pray tell," he said.

Tom shuffled around a little. "When Mary and I, you know…" he said, pumping his fist tight to his chest so no one else could see. "She kind of gets a little excited and a little loud, when we're at her parents' house or my mother's we have to well…" Tom started to look uncomfortable.

"You have to what?" asked Wil, stifling a laugh.

"Mary puts a pillow over her face to muffle the moans," said Tom. "At least when we're in the house no one can hear us, but a thin tent everyone will hear."

"Wow, you stud," said Wil. "It looks like it's the pillow again then my friend." He patted his friend on the back and moved off to grab his pack and his belongings.

Tom cursed under his breath, "If I'd have known I would have asked to stay at your house while you lot came up here," he said to himself.

The six friends moved off, Vanessa taking the lead while Wil brought up the rear. He turned and looked back at the now deserted farmyard and wondered what had happened to the farm where he had spent so many summers. He felt Rochelle tug on his arm and they moved on.

Chapter four

Wil was woken by his alarm clock, he could already hear movement downstairs. The fifteen-year-old dressed quickly, opened his bedroom door and hurried down the stairs. As he entered the kitchen the smell of Morag's cooking filled his nostrils, his stomach rumbled. "Good morning to you young William," said Morag. "I hope you woke with an appetite!"

"I always do," he said grinning and taking a seat at the table. Morag placed a plate of bacon, sausage, beans, eggs, tomatoes, and fried bread in front of him with a pint of fresh orange juice. Wil thanked her and started to devour the food. Vanessa walked into the kitchen still rubbing her eyes, kissed Morag on the cheek, took the coffee that was offered to her and sat at the table. She looked at her brother who had egg yolk running down his chin.

"God you're a pig," she said. "Wipe your chin." Wil's arm came up and he wiped away the yolk with his sleeve then smiled at his sister. She stuck her tongue out at him then took the plate of breakfast from Morag.

"Oh, leave him be, lass," said Morag. "I love to see a man with a good appetite." She walked past Wil and ruffled his hair.

"There is a difference between a good appetite and

greed," said Vanessa. "My brother here could out eat your pigs, not just one, all of them."

Angus walked in the kitchen. "You're only saying that because you eat like a sparrow. I hope young William has left some breakfast for me." He took a seat at the table and Morag set his plate in front of him, adding two more sausages to Wil's plate. Wil looked up and smiled broadly at her.

"God, woman, you spoil that boy. Where is my extra sausage?" he said winking at the twins.

"He is a growing boy and he'll be doing all the heavy work while you stand there and say 'oh, my back'." Vanessa let out a chuckle as Morag berated her husband.

When she finished, Angus looked at the twins and winked. "She loves me really. Come on young William, let's be getting those cows out to the fields so they can eat," said Angus, standing and passing the empty plate to his wife. Wil handed Morag his own plate and thanked her with a kiss to the cheek. As he walked past his sister, he stole the last sausage off her plate then ran out the door.

"Greedy pig!" she shouted after him.

Angus shook his head and laughed. "That boy is a delight. Vanessa my dear, will you do the chicken pens and collect the eggs please." He kissed his wife and followed Wil out the door.

Vanessa sipped her coffee. "Have you heard anything from my dad?" she asked Morag.

"No sweetie, nothing yet. I'm sure he's fine. Angus always said your dad was one of the best he'd ever served with. Said that man could find his way through any problem that came at him."

"I know he can," said Vanessa. "But I hate it when he has to go on these missions. I always fear he won't come home."

Morag walked over and put her arms around her. "Now look here," she said. "Your father will be back before you know it and he and my Angus will swap stories of where they've been and what nonsense they got up to. Just you wait and see. Now be off with you so I can get the bread in the oven for dinner, we're having beef stew with dumplings."

"I hope you made enough to fill the black hole that is my brother," said Vanessa as she headed out of the kitchen. "I still say he could eat more than all your pigs put together."

Wil sat on the quad as the last of the cows went through the gate to the field. Angus swung the gate shut and walked over to the young lad. "Come with me," he said. "But don't tell Morag we goofed off for an hour."

Angus set off to the barn. Wil followed when Angus said "goofing off", it always meant something fun was about to happen. The last time he said "let's do something fun" Wil was handed a shotgun and he and Angus had blown off the heads of scarecrows. That was until Morag found them and had at length told Angus how stupid he was for letting a fourteen-year-old use a shotgun. "God, woman, be calm." Angus had tried to argue back. "This is the gun his father saved my life with."

"I don't care if he saved the queen of bloody England with it, he's just a wee boy and you need to remember that!" What Morag didn't know is that Wil had been shown how to handle a variety of weapons by his father and was quite the marksman. Wil was excited to see what Angus had got in store for him today. As they entered the barn, a straw dummy had been set up by the far wall. Angus ushered the lad inside and looked around to make sure Morag wasn't looking. From behind a bale of hay Angus pulled out a bow and handed it to Wil.

"Have you ever used one of these, lad?" asked Angus.

"No," replied Wil trying to hold down his excitement.

"Take the arrow and notch it in the bow, draw it back to your cheek, take aim and let it fly at the target."

Wil followed as instructed, the arrow shot through the air and punch home into the head of the dummy. "Not bad," said Angus.

"I was aiming for his chest," replied Wil.

Angus let out a huge laugh. "Well, at least you're honest," he said. This time release your breath as you loose the arrow."

Wil notched a second arrow, drew in a breath and let it fly. The arrow hit dead centre on the painted target, he turned and looked at Angus, a huge smile on his face. "Try another," said Angus,

Wil loosed anther arrow, that hit only centimetres away from the first. "By heavens boy, you're a natural. Now this is known as the silent killer, mine and your dad's preferred choice when we're being covert. No sound and deadly. This is now yours, practice with as much as you like in here, just don't let Morag see you otherwise I'm in for another ear bashing. God, I think that woman's tongue is more deadly than the bow," he added.

Wil laughed at him. "Why is it you and Morag never had kids?" he asked the man. Angus laid his hand on Wil's shoulder and looked the powerful youth in the eye.

"Morag is barren Wil. We would have loved kids of our own but we can't, that's why we love it when you and your sister come and stay with us. If I'd have had a son like you, God only knows how proud and happy that would have made me. When you two were born your dad was in my regiment under my command, he was so excited when you were born. We were both away on a mission when you came along, your mother brought you both here and Morag helped your mother for the first few weeks until your father and I got back. So, in a way I do have kids, you and your sister are the kids Morag and I never had, that's why she loves you so much. Now let's stop the mushy stuff, we have work to do and if she finds us in here, she'll be on at us both."

Wil loved it at the farm, everything had a routine and he was free to help out with anything and he was treated as an adult there by Angus. Although Morag kept an eye on him like a mother hen. Wil knew that his father would be home soon and that they would go to the cabin as they always did and that would be the end of the summer on the farm.

Vanessa however seemed none too bothered when it came time to go home. She loved the busy life the hustle and bustle, it was okay when you didn't stand out like a sore thumb. At fifteen Wil stood at six feet tall and was heavily muscled. He was already stronger than most men, his father had pushed him to his physical limits and still

Will had surpassed these, every time, wanting to be stronger. Something inside, drove him onwards. The days were long on the farm and every spare moment he had, Wil would sneak off to the barn and practice with the bow. He had just sighted the target, took in his breath ready to fire when a voice cut through his concentration. He released the arrow which thudded into the barn wall, splintering wood.

He turned to see his sister sitting high on the hay bales. "So, this is where you've been sneaking off to," she said climbing down.

"Christ, Ness, you scared me half to death. What are you doing in here?" he asked.

"I've seen you sneaking off and got curious. "Can I have a go?"

Wil handed her the bow. "Angus said not to let Morag find out." He showed her how to hold the bow and instructed her how to use it. The first few arrows missed the dummy but Vanessa persisted and after half an hour she could hit the target.

"This is fun," she exclaimed. "Do we have something better to shoot at?"

Wil looked at her. "I'm going down in the fields later with it, I want to see if I can get a few rabbits."

"I'll come with you," said his sister. "We can say we want to go for a walk together if Morag asks."

Wil nodded his agreement. "Okay meet me here just after the evening meal," he told her.

The twins sat in silence in the field. Wil had uprooted a small bush that they sat behind for cover. Vanessa was growing bored. "How long will this take?" she asked getting irritated.

"It will take longer if you're not quiet," he hissed under his breath. Just then a couple of rabbits came into view, Wil notched the arrow, drew back the bow and calmly released. The rabbit was shot through the head and died instantly, the other ran back towards the safety of the brambles. As Wil went over to retrieve his arrow, Vanessa looked at her brother.

"I don't think I will have a go at that," she said. "I feel so sad that we killed it."

"Well, I don't," said Wil. "I'll enjoy eating this, I can't wait to show Angus."

The twins set off back to the farmhouse talking quietly to each other. As they came round the corner of the last farm building Vanessa froze then set off at a sprint. It took Wil a moment to see what she had seen. There in front of the farmhouse was a car. Their father's car. Wil set off at a sprint trying to catch up with his sister, just as they reached the door it opened. Vanessa flew into her father's arms sobbing. Alex held his daughter for a few heart beats then said, "It's all right, I'm home now."

She stepped back wiping the tears away. Wil stepped forward and embraced his father in a bear hug. "Whoa steady there, son, are you trying to break my back?"

Wil stepped back, his eyes glinting with tears. "It is good to see you, dad," he said, his voice betraying his emotions.

"Look at you my boy, you get bigger every time I see you. And you, Vanessa, could you be any more beautiful?" He embraced both his children again. "Come inside, I have something to tell you both."

They were all sat at the table, apart from Alex who stood in the kitchen, still in his uniform. His black hair had been shaved close to his head and hints of silver could be seen. The silver hair was more visible in his close-cropped goatee beard. "As you all know, the army has been my life for a long time now, and being in the SAS has taken me to places to do things I'll never forget. This mission I've just got back from…" He paused for a couple of seconds. "This was my last mission for the army. I'm retiring." Vanessa jumped from her chair and hugged her father, tears of joy falling to her cheeks. She sobbed openly with joy.

Angus walked over to his friend and embraced him. "Well, it's about bloody time, man, I'm happy for you." He turned to his wife. "Morag, my love, get the whisky out, this calls for a celebration."

Wil heard his name being called; it was Vanessa. "Can we rest a while? Not everyone is as fit as you."

"Speak for yourself," said Tom through ragged breaths, dropping to the floor.

Wil removed his pack. "Okay guys, take five. But don't drink too much water, it will only give you a stitch."

As the others sat down Wil turned to Rochelle. "Stay with the others, I'll be back soon."

"Why? Where are you going?" she asked him.

"Don't worry," he told her. "The campsite is only another hour away I'll move on ahead and start preparing things for you guys."

She held on to his hand. "Be careful," she said smiling sweetly at him.

He winked back. "I always am. Do me a favour?" he

said. "Stay with Brad, he's struggling and I think that Smithy is starting to annoy him."

"I will," she promised. Wil took the tents from the others and set off on his own. Tom watched his friend lope off.

"And where is Mr Olympia off to now?" he asked.

"He said he was going ahead to start setting up the campsite for us," answered Rochelle.

Tom stood, hands on hips, breathing heavily still. "Wonderful," he said. "Tell me, Rochelle, how do you keep up with him? I mean I love the guy to bits but does he ever rest?"

Rochelle stood, walked to Tom and patted his cheek. "No, he never rests till I'm completely satisfied, then I let him sleep. Maybe you should try doing the same for Mary." She turned and winked at Mary who burst out laughing, the others joined in. Tom blushed as the others set off walking after Wil.

Tom looked at his girlfriend. "I satisfy you right, babe?" he said weakly.

"Yes, you do," she answered back hiding a smile. John had dropped back to walk with his friend Dave while Vanessa and Rochelle along with Brad were in the lead, walking steady.

"Did you hear that back there?" asked Dave. "Man, I bet that Rochelle is a demon in the sack."

John laughed. "Sadly, my friend, you'll never find out and if by chance you ever did, I don't think you'd live long enough to tell the tale."

Wil had been growing impatient of the pace set by the others. Now he had set off at a steady run, filling his lungs with the clear highland air. The camp site where they would stay wasn't far but Wil was eager to get there and get things set up. He soon found the place where they would stay the night. The camp area was situated at the top of a gently sloped hill that led down to a small loch. Quickly he erected the tents and set the stones for the fire and lit it. Dropping his pack inside his tent he quickly unpacked his bow, grabbed the arrows and strapped on his survival knife. A final check on the campsite and he was off in search of dinner.

The group crested the hill to find a flat area where Wil had pitched their tents, the campsite looked down on a small loch the sun was just starting to set, turning the water of the loch to gold. A small fire had been set in a circle of stones and a note was pinned to Wil's tent. Vanessa walked over, took the note and read it aloud. "Gone to catch dinner, be back soon. Be careful the water is cold."

"What does he mean?" asked Brad. "Gone to catch dinner? What are we having?"

"I honestly don't know, Bradley. It could be anything from rabbit to pheasant or even fish, but I don't see him at the loch so probably rabbit."

The others set about unpacking their packs, Vanessa and Mary walked down to the loch to fill the water canteens from the natural spring that fed it. Wil came walking back carrying five dead rabbits that he had skinned and gutted. Soon the smell of roasting meat filled the air as Wil spit roasted the rabbits. The others had opened a few cans of beer and there was a sense of enjoyment as they sat and ate, the night was clear and cloudless as the friends talked.

Tom and Mary stood up and walked off. "We're just going for a little walk," said Tom.

Wil looked over at his friend. "Keep the firelight in site, don't get lost out there."

"We won't," shouted Mary. Five minutes later the cries of "oh yes Tom" could be heard laughter filled the campsite.

"Didn't you tell him that sound carried further up here?" Vanessa asked her brother.

"Nope," replied Wil laughing. Mary's groaning grew louder and louder then finally stopped. A few minutes later Tom and Mary came walking back into the campsite.

With a straight face Dave asked, "Did you have a nice walk?"

"We had a lovely walk," replied Mary. "Well, I'm tired now so I think I'll go to bed." With that she entered her tent. Tom sat beside Brad and looked at the grinning faces of the others.

"What's everyone looking at me for?" he asked.

Brad leant in close. "We heard you," he whispered. Tom blushed. "Wil didn't tell you about the echo up here?"

Tom stood. "I told you she was satisfied!" he said, turned on his heels and joined Mary in the tent.

"Well," said Wil stretching. "I think I'll follow suit and hit the hay."

Rochelle held out her hand and he pulled her to her feet. "Night all," they both said and disappeared into their tent. The night was warm. Wil removed his trousers and t-shirt, folding them he laid them to one side, Rochelle had closed the front of the tent and was kneeling looking at her boyfriend. Slowly she unzipped her top then lifted her t-shirt off to reveal a red lace bra. She tossed the t-shirt at Wil, then she removed her trousers to reveal a matching red thong. Slowly she unhooked the bra exposing her firm ample breasts. She reached back and untied her hair, letting it fall to her shoulders. Wil's heart was beating fast as Rochelle dropped to all fours and started to crawl towards him.

As she straddled his body, she ran her hands up over his powerful chest. Wil reached out and cupped her breasts, softly pinching the nipple. She moaned with pleasure at his touch, her nipples hardening. Slowly she moved back and forth on his groin, feeling him swell. One of his hands slid down her body and between her legs. Carefully he slipped one of his fingers inside her, her moaning intensified. She moved back and forth faster, her body quivering with delight. She leant forward and kissed him, her lips tasted sweet upon his. Rochelle reached down into his boxers and he entered her.

Their love making was what they both needed at that point, being together the freedom of the hike, the love they shared for one another. Rochelle finally climaxed throwing her head back. Wil quickly turned her over, he was now on top. He could feel her surrender to him completely, his love making intensified and she moaned even more. Rochelle was in ecstasy, she climaxed again digging her fingernails into Wil's back. The pain was pleasurable. Then, he too climaxed. They both lay there sweat drenched and panting for breath. Wil rolled from her and her arm draped across his body, sleep came instantly for both of them.

Chapter Five

Alex had been retired now for a well over a year and spent his days working in his garden. The twins were approaching their eighteenth birthday, Vanessa had taken a job working for a cosmetics company and was exceling at the job. Wil had said he wanted to go to college to study engineering. Alex was happy that neither of them had wanted to join the army. Wil was training harder and harder gaining muscle all the time. Alex couldn't believe how strong his son was, he had watched him train the other day in the home gym. Wil had placed two hundred kilograms on the bar and bench pressed it ten times. Even in his prime Alex couldn't match him. Vanessa had become so independent — he had been truly blessed with his children.

He sighed, if only their mother had lived to see them grow, she would have been so proud. He remembered it like it was yesterday the night of the accident. The twins had been sleeping and Laura had just popped out to go shopping. "Love you," she had said. "Won't be long." Those were the last words she had spoken. The driver of the other car was three times over the limit and had hit Laura's car on the driver's side at seventy miles per hour. She had died instantly, the other driver they found clinging to life.

Alex had gone numb when the police officer had told him — time seemed to stand still. When he had looked back at the officer, he seemed huge, then Alex realized he had dropped to his knees. He had taken compassionate leave from the army and headed to Scotland where Angus and Morag had helped out with the kids. Alex had never been the same from that day, something inside of him had died. Vanessa was the spitting image of her mother and as much as he loved her it brought a sense of pain when he looked at his daughter.

He heard the gate close and saw his son stride into the garden. "Fancy a work out, Dad?" he had said.

"No, son," replied Alex. "I have a headache again."

"You should get that checked out," said Wil.

"I will do son. Don't worry. Come on, let's see if you can beat that two-hundred-kilogram press."

Life was good, his children were happy, he was home for good — no more missions to take him away, then tragedy had struck. Alex had collapsed in the garden one day and had died instantly. Vanessa had found him there, she had come home from work early to find him laid face down, his body cold. She had dialled nine-nine-nine then called her brother. Wil had run out of college, nearly taking the door off its hinges as he wrenched it open. As he got to the house the paramedics were just loading his father's body into the ambulance. Wil started to push the paramedics out of the way trying to get to his father. One of the attending police officers had tried to restrain him but ended up being thrown out of the way. It was only the voice of his sister that had cut through his pain and sorrow that brought him to his senses. He had collapsed to his knees his sister hugging him, both of them had cried openly in the street.

Wil awoke, his mouth dry, looking at his watch it was six a.m. Gently he removed Rochelle's arm from his body, grabbing his towel from his pack he strode off down to the loch. He stood on a jutting boulder and dove head first into the water. He swam for a few seconds underneath the surface, enjoying the coolness of the water. As he broke to the surface, he took in a huge lung full of air and swam for shore, he towelled himself down then returned to the campsite. Everyone else was still sleeping. He dressed quickly grabbed his fishing gear and returned to the loch.

The smell of cooking fish greeted the nostrils of everyone in their tents. Rochelle's hand snaked out reaching for Wil, but as usual he was up and out. Sleepily she dressed and came out of the tent. There, crouched in front of the campfire, was Wil cooking the fish. Her stomach rumbled as the smell hit her. "Good morning," she greeted him.

Looking up he smiled. As she approached, she pushed him back, making him sit on the floor. She sat over him kissing him deeply. "I hope you're hungry!" he said.

"Starving," she answered.

A cough from behind made them both look. The rest of the group had emerged from their tents and were all looking at the roasting fish. "Would you two care to be alone?" asked Tom.

Rochelle blushed. "Just saying good morning to my man," she told him standing up.

"I wish she would say good morning to me," whispered Dave in John's ear.

They sat and ate the breakfast Wil had prepared, then the three girls headed off to the loch for a swim while the others broke camp ready to move on to the next site. Tom constantly watched Dave, his eyes lingering on the three girls swimming. He kept leaning in and whispering in John's ear, then they would both laugh.

Tom approached Wil. "Have you seen how he keeps looking over? It's starting to piss me off."

"Relax," said Wil. "I'll talk with him if it carries on."

"It's not just Mary he's ogling, I've seen him watching Rochelle too."

"I know," answered Wil, putting a reassuring hand on his friend's shoulder. "Just chill out. Mary hasn't shown any interest back so what's the problem? And from what we heard last night no one could match you! You being the stallion that you are."

Tom blushed and started to laugh. "That was a shitty thing to do bro. You could have warned me about the echo."

With a straight face Wil looked at his friend. "What, and rob every one of the entertainment? I don't think so." Then he burst out laughing. "Come on, help me pack up so we can reach the next site."

Vanessa, Mary and Rochelle had returned from their swim and quickly dressed. The six companions set off once more. They had been gone for around an hour when a huge black form entered the camp site. It sniffed at the fire pit which caused the creature to sneeze. Its huge head moved from side to side sniffing the air. With the scent of the camp filling is nostrils it ambled over towards a small bush where it found the fish guts that had been thrown away. These, it ate quickly, its great head came up as it caught the scent from the people in the distance and set off in pursuit of its next meal.

Chapter six

Wil and his friends had walked for a few hours now and the complaints had started. "How long till we get there?"

"My feet hurt, can we stop for a rest?"

Wil's favourite one was, "I thought you said this would be fun!"

Wil had promised them that when they got to the next campsite that they would have more fun as they could break out the beer and Wil would treat them to the vacuum-packed steaks he had brought along. This seemed to quieten the complainers. When they had set camp once again Vanessa took charge of the cooking. The smell from the steak had everyone's mouth-watering, the beer was opened and the music was turned on and they all relaxed. Even Brad seemed to be enjoying himself. Wil picked up his bow and knife and told Rochelle he would be back shortly.

Dave had seen Wil leave the camp. Looking over at his friend he said, "There goes Rambo."

John laughed aloud. "Fucking Rambo. Don't push me," he said a little too loud. John met Vanessa's gaze, the look she gave him was chilling. He knew she wasn't happy as she stood and left the campsite. "Bollocks!" swore John. "That's me not getting any tonight."

The others had seen the exchange — an

uncomfortable silence fell over the rest of them. "I'll go and talk to her," said Brad, standing and leaving before anyone could say anything. He found Vanessa a short distance away sitting on a large rock staring out over the hills. The sun was just starting to set, casting its golden glow over the highlands. "Is it okay if I join you?" he asked smiling.

Vanessa moved over and Brad sat beside her. "It's beautiful out here," she said as he sat down.

"Are you okay?" he asked.

She looked at him and her words shocked him. "Why does John act like such a prick every time he has a drink? His mouth gets him in trouble. I don't want any friction on this trip, it means so much to Wil and I..." She paused for a second. "If Wil heard him, I know what Wil could do to a prick like John. So you remember last time? Wil broke John's jaw."

Brad gave out a small chuckle. Vanessa looked at him. "Sorry," said Brad. "But I enjoyed hearing about that." Vanessa put her arm around Brad's back and leant her head on his shoulder. Brad could smell the perfume on her and started to feel uncomfortable. His heart was pounding and his breathing quickened. He shifted his weight, Vanessa lifted her head. Brad knew that this was his moment to act.

He had gone over this a thousand times in his head. His first real kiss with the woman he loved. He leant forward, his lips touching hers, and for a second, she kissed him back. Then she pulled away, a look of shock on her face.

"What are you doing?" she asked him.

80

"I love you, Vanessa. I always have ever since we were kids. I've loved you for so many years. You deserve so much better than John. I overheard him telling Smithy that he's been seeing someone else while you're away and that after this trip he's going to end it with you."

Vanessa stood up. "What are you saying? What's going on?"

"I'll tell you what's going on," came the voice of John from behind them. "That fat little prick is trying to steal you from me. I've seen how he follows you around like a lost puppy." John stepped forward pushing Brad from where he sat on the rock. "Well fat boy, what are you going to do now? Make up more lies about me? I love Vanessa so back the fuck off."

Vanessa stood in front of Brad who was still laid on the floor. "Enough John!" she snapped at him. "Leave him alone!"

Brad got to his feet. "It's not a lie, I heard telling Smithy at the services. You were bragging about it to him."

John lunged forward pushing Brad making him stumble. "Liar!" shouted John.

Vanessa stepped in once more. "John, I know he's not lying, I found an earring in your bed. I was going to end it with you," she told him. John looked shocked. "Brad's right," she continued. "I do deserve better than you."

Brad took a step forward to stand at her side. John's arm flashed up delivering an uppercut to Brad's chin. He went down like he'd been poleaxed.

Vanessa stepped forward slapping John across the face. "You're an arsehole, John, and when Wil gets back,

I won't be standing in his way. He's going to kick the living shit out of you."

John grabbed her by her neck. "I'm not scared of your brother, Smithy and I can handle him," he said, no confidence in his voice. "I'm glad you found out," he continued. "Do you think I want to be at home waiting for you to get back? I have needs, I need a real woman."

Pushing her back, she fell over the unconscious Brad. "That's you all over John, acting the big man when you've had a drink. Keep walking away John, I can't wait until my brother gets back!" shouted Vanessa.

She turned, kneeling and started to pat Brad's cheek. "Bradley, can you hear me? Come on Brad, wake up!" Brad moaned. "That's it," said Vanessa. "Wake up!"

Brad opened his eyes. "What happened?" he asked slowly rubbing his jaw.

"John hit you," she told him. "Are you okay?" Slowly Brad got to his feet, he felt the nausea hit him and he staggered a little. Vanessa took hold of him. "Steady," she told him.

"I'm okay," he said. "I know I'm not the most handsome of men Vanessa but I do love you and I would never hurt you like John has."

Vanessa took a deep breath. "Brad, I love you too but not in that way. I see you more as a little brother." She reached out to hold his hand but he took a step back from her.

"Please don't be like that," she asked him.

"I just want to be alone," he told her. He turned and walked away.

"Bradley, wait! It's getting dark, you'll get lost!" she

called after him.

Without turning he shouted back, "I'll be fine, just give me some space." With a heavy heart Vanessa headed back to the campsite.

Wil quietly finished. Another rabbit snare movement to his right made him look up quickly, nothing there. Something made him take a second look. What was that through the trees? The light was fading. He picked up his bow and moved towards it. Whatever it was it was big. As he emerged from the trees Wil stood there in disbelief at what he was looking at. Trees had been uprooted and smashed to shards, the ground had been churned up. Some kind of craft had crashed into the woods, a huge gaping hole had been torn in its side when the ship had crashed. Wil slowly moved forward, bow drawn ready.

Looking round Wil knelt down and inspected the ground. It had been there for about three weeks. Cautiously Wil moved forward towards the opening and stopped to listen. After a few minutes he heard nothing then entered the craft, slinging his bow he drew his hunting knife. Cautiously he moved through the wreckage deeper into the ship. Outside a black silhouette moved and scented the ground where Wil had been stood. Letting out a low growl it moved off into the shadows.

Inside the ship, Wil entered what he assumed was the flight deck. Wires hung down from all over, the ship was smashed to pieces and in the middle a single chair with the remains of the pilot ripped to pieces. The only light in the ship came from a single, green flashing light. Wil moved forward sheathing his knife and laying his bow on the floor. He moved towards the flashing light, it seemed to part of some kind of control panel. In front of the flashing light was a recess in the metal in the shape of a hand print — a hand print Wil nor anyone else had never seen before. Clearly, he could see the thumb digit, but there was only space for another three fingers. Placing his fore finger and middle finger together he placed his hand in the recess.

Instantly a dome snapped shut around his wrist, his hand started to go warm. Pain ran through his body as the ship interfaced with him. Images of the ship's travel log and history ran through his mind as if he had been on that ship. He saw the pilot pinned in his seat, the black creature moving in for the kill. Images raced through his mind, a sense of nausea threatened to overwhelm him. He started to sway but his hand remained fixed in place. He saw the ship hit by the meteor that caused it to crash, then the image changed. Wil saw the ship on an alien world with two suns in a purple sky, the pilot loading in the terrible beasts. The image shifted again, this time he was on another planet inside a huge stadium, lizard-like humanoids dressed in armour carrying swords and axes. Then the release of the Kray-loth — a black beast with six limbs and razor-sharp talons. The beast was huge and hairless, it had an extended maw which ended in a beak-like hook, the head had an extended crown of black bone that swept back over its head, ridged scales ran down its back that ended on its short tail, its front legs were heavily muscled and armoured with black scales, and huge wide powerful shoulders, its black skin shone like silk. It looked at its tormenters, the lizard warriors spread out to do combat against the Kray-loth — ten warriors against one Kray-loth.

The beast darted forward, taking out the first warrior with one swing of its talons. The watching crowd cheered as he died, another ran in burring his axe into the back of the Kray-loth. With a back-handed slash the second warrior died, two more ran in to stab at the beast. It spun on one of its attackers, sinking its beak-like mouth into his shoulder. With a snap of its head the lizard man was sent flying through the air. Other warriors ran in, throwing spears and slashing at the Kray-loth with swords. Two small arms came from under its chest as it grabbed hold of one of the attackers, lifting him from the ground. Frantically the lizard man tried to escape as the huge mouth closed on his head, time and time again the Kray-loth took more injuries as sword, axe and spear took their damage on the beast. Finally, its great strength giving out it slumped to the floor. Only a few of its attackers remained. Weakly it lashed out as one ran in for the death blow, its attacker fell back trying to hold in his entrails. Pain seared through the Kray-loth as another spear was thrown into its side, its great head dropped to the arena floor then darkness greeted it. Two of the lizard men stood holding aloft the head of the Kray-loth.

The dome around Wil's wrist released him, darkness swamped him as he fell backwards losing consciousness. From out of the dark came a woman, she moved to Wil's side and checked his pulse, it was beating strong. Looking round she picked up the knife and waited. Wil opened his eyes, the flashing green light had stopped, he was in complete darkness. He was aware that someone or something was beside him. Slowly he felt round for his knife.

"It's okay," came a voice. "I have your knife." Wil turned his head, situated in the dark he could make out the shape of a woman.

"Who are you?" he asked.

"I'm Amanda," she answered. Wil tried to sit, his head spun, forcing him to lay back down.

"How long have I been out?" he asked her.

"About an hour, I think," she told him. Wil tried again to stand, dizziness forced him to grab hold of the woman.

"What are you doing here, Amanda?" he asked her.

"We were attacked back at our campsite, something killed all of my friends. I managed to escape. I just ran and ran. I came upon this ship yesterday and I've been hiding here ever since." She handed Wil his knife. "What happened when you touched the green light? You started to thrash around and then you spoke in a language I've never heard."

Wil shook his head. "I don't fully understand what happened, yet I'm getting images in my mind. I have to get back to my friends," he told her.

"Wait!" she screamed. "You can't go out there! That thing is out there!"

"You mean the Kray-loth," he said.

She looked at him. "How do you know what it's called?"

Wil rubbed his head. "The ship told me, I think. Look, I have to get back to my friends, you can come with me. I'll keep you safe," he told her, holding out his hand.

Amanda took a step backwards. "I don't know," she said, her voice breaking and tears falling to her cheek.

"Stay here if you want but I have to get back to my friends and warn them." He turned to leave then looked back at her. "Come with me please. We have food and there's safety in numbers."

Amanda stood still for a moment. Wil set off to move. "Wait!" she cried. "Who are you?"

"I'm Wil," he said. Looking back and holding out his hand, Amanda stepped forward and took the outstretched hand. Together they made their way out of the ship and set off back to the campsite to warn his friends.

Chapter seven

Vanessa sat with Rochelle, glaring at John. There was an uncomfortable silence in the camp. Mary stood and turned on the music. "Wil's been gone a long time, hasn't he? Do you think he's okay?" asked Rochelle.

Vanessa smiled. "Don't worry. Wil knows this place like the back of his hand, he'll be fine."

John came walking over. "Can we talk?" he asked Vanessa.

"There's nothing to talk about," she replied.

"I just want to say sorry," he told her.

"I'm not the only one you should say sorry too. You need to apologize to Brad," she snapped.

"I will," he stammered back. "As soon as the little guy comes back, I'll say sorry."

Vanessa stood a look of concern on her face. "I should never have let him go off. It's easy to get lost out here."

Dave joined in the conversation. "Where is the little guy? I'll go and find him."

"No!" said Vanessa. "You could get lost too. We'll wait for Wil to get back, he'll find him."

Brad could hear the music and see the soft glow of the camp fire in the distance. His jaw hurt from the punch but hunger and feeling a little cold had made him swallow his pride and turn around. A low growl came from behind which made him freeze in his tracks. He slowly turned. Another growl, this time to his left, but closer to him this time. Brad could see the firelight in the distance. Another growl from the right — panic set in. He started to run, terror stopping him from calling out. Tom looked around.

"Brad's never been much of an outdoor person, I hope he's okay."

"He'll be fine," said John.

"He'd be fine if you hadn't hit him!" snapped Tom.

"Wait a minute, he kissed Nessa and I hit him once," said John defensively.

"You're a fucking prick, John!" snapped Tom. "Brad hasn't got a fight in him. Trust you to pick on the smallest guy here.

"I could pick on you if you'd like, Tom," said John stepping forward.

"Just stop it for God's sake," snapped Vanessa. "Brad's missing, that's what's important right now."

Brad was now running frantically. He kept glimpsing a dark shadow to his right. He could now hear the music in the campsite clearly. One hundred yards away from the safety of the camp. Brad was set upon by the Kray-loth, with one swipe of its paw Brad's head toppled to the ground, his body took three faltering steps, then it too fell. The Kray-loth stood over the body, its tongue snaking out to lap up the blood. An ungodly howl cut through the arguing.

"What was that?" asked Mary, stepping closer to Tom.

"I don't know," replied Vanessa. She felt Rochelle

take hold of her hand.

"Where's Wil?" she whispered in Vanessa's ear.

"I don't know," Vanessa whispered back. The six of them stood still for a few more heartbeats, then Dave let out a laugh. All eyes turned on him.

"It's obvious what's going on," he said. "Wil bumped into Brad on his way back hear told him that he'd been in an argument with John and now Wil is trying to scare us all."

"No," said Vanessa stepping forward. "I know my brother and he wouldn't mess around out here."

"Dave's right," agreed John. "It's Wil and Brad trying to scare us!" Grabbing a torch, he walked past Vanessa and the others. "Come on Dave, let's go and spoil their fun."

"It's not my brother!" snapped Vanessa. He wouldn't mess around like that."

The two men ignored her and carried on walking in the direction of the howl. John turned to his friend. "Look man, I may need you to help me if Wil starts on me."

Dave looked at his friend. "Are you serious? I don't think I'd be much help. That Wil is one big fucker, and from what you've told me, it will take more than you and me, to take him on."

"Look," said John. "You just need to…" he paused mid-sentence.

"I need to what?" asked Dave. He turned and looked at his friend who had come to a standstill. John was visibly shaking. "John, what's the matter with you?" Slowly John's hand came up pointing. Dave turned his gaze to where John pointed. There on the floor in a pool of blood lay Brad's head, his eyes and mouth fixed in an expression of fear. Dave let out a cry and jumped back. "What the fuck man, that's his fucking head."

Dave looked round in every direction then noticed his friend was still rooted to the spot. "John, come on we have to go back! John, come on man, snap out of it!" Dave grabbed the torch. As he took hold of it he heard movement causing him to swing the light in the direction. What greeted him was a huge hulking monster stood glaring at them, blood dripping from its mouth, Brad's mutilated body in front of it. John let out a scream of terror, he shone the light directly into the eyes of the Kray-loth which scooped up the body and ran off.

John felt hands grab him, pulling at him, a slap to the face brought him out of the shocked state. "Move you fucking idiot! Move!" he heard Dave shouting at him. Then he was moving, his legs felt heavy as he stumbled along. He could see the light from the fire which made him run faster. Both men entered the campsite, John's face drained of all colour.

Vanessa stepped forward. "What's wrong? What happened?"

Gasping for breath, Dave managed to say, "Brad's dead, something killed him!"

Tom looked at the two men who now stood hands on hips, taking in deep gulping breaths. "Wait, what do you mean Brad's dead?" he said, his voice shaky.

"What do you think he means!" snapped John. "Brad's fucking dead! His head is over there on the fucking floor in a pool of his blood."

"No, he can't be," said Tom looking at Vanessa.

"Look if you don't believe me go and look," said John pointing in the direction he had come from.

"Wait a minute, just hold on," commanded Vanessa. "What could have possibly killed Brad?"

"I don't know," interrupted Dave. "But whatever it was it was huge. It had black skin, blood dripping from its mouth, it just grabbed Brad's body and disappeared."

"What else can you tell me about it?" Vanessa pressed him for more information. "How big was it?"

"I don't know," stammered Dave. "About this big," he said, holding his hand just below his chin. "It happened so quickly; its shoulders were huge it just scooped up Brad's body like it was carrying a child. What do you think it was?" Dave asked her.

"I have no idea," she replied.

"So, what do we do now?" asked Tom. All eyes turned on Vanessa.

"We do nothing," came Wil's voice. The six of them turned to see Wil stood silhouetted in the firelight, a young woman at his side. Instantly Rochelle was in his arms.

"I thought you weren't coming back," she told him through tears.

Vanessa approached her brother. "Brad's gone," she told him. Looking at the woman with him, "Who's this with you?"

"This is Amanda. Where's Brad's body?" he asked.

"Gone," said Dave. "That thing took it, it's about a hundred yards that way."

"Build up the fire," said Wil. "The light should keep them away, especially if they've fed."

"Wil you said them. How many of them are out there, and how do you know?" asked Tom pushing past Dave.

"Build up the fire and I'll tell you."

John frantically built up the fire, constantly scanning around. "While I was out setting traps, I caught the sight of something through the trees just as the light was fading. I was just getting ready to come back." Wil paused for a second. "It's an alien ship guys. It's crash landed, and looking at the surroundings I'd say it happened about three weeks ago. Those two creatures where on board being transported—"

Tom interrupted his friend. "Wait a minute. How do you know this?"

"I went into that ship to look around. What was left of the pilot is still in there, but it's been ripped to pieces. The only thing that was working was a flashing light. When I touched it the ship's memory must have linked with me, like a recording of some kind. Those two creatures are like some kind of arena animal that they bring in to fight as a rite of passage."

"Who brings what to fight?" asked Tom.

"From what I learnt in the ship those things out there are called Kray-loths and the others that fight them are called the Mojave. They are like a big lizard but stand up straight like a human. The ship is where I found Amanda, the Kray-loth came upon her camp a couple of days ago and killed her friends. She managed to escape."

"Now just hold a minute there. Aliens, spaceships, monsters… What the fuck man? This was supposed to be a few days of fun and now fucking alien monsters are out there trying to kill us!" shouted Tom. "What the fuck are we going to do?"

"I'll tell you what we do. We go take some pictures of that ship, grab something as proof. Get back to the farm and get the fuck out of here," said Dave.

"Why do we need pictures?" asked John.

"Dude, it's a fucking real alien ship. We'll be rich!"

"No!" interrupted Wil. "You'll be dead. Those creatures out there will hunt you down before you make it back to the farm."

"What do we do Wil? Come on man you're the survival expert!" asked Tom.

"Get some sleep, we'll keep watch! Nessa, John and Dave take first watch. Rochelle and I will take the second and you and Mary take the third."

"What about me?" asked Amanda. "I can help."

"No," said Wil. "You're exhausted, have something to eat then take Brad's tent and get some rest. In the morning we make for the cabin, there's a CB radio there. We can bunker down and call for help, it's our best chance for survival."

"Wait a minute," said John. "You want to go further away from the farm and the van? What the fuck man!"

Vanessa interrupted. "He's right guys! The farm is a full day's hike away from here. The cabin is only half that distance."

"Wait, what about Wil going on his own?" asked Tom. "If he was on his own, he wouldn't have us to slow him down. He could make it and Vanessa could take the rest of us to the cabin."

"Just hold on a god damn minute!" snapped Rochelle. "If you think that I'm going to let Wil sacrifice himself on his own out there you're crazy."

"Look the best way for us to survive is to stay together strength in numbers, these things have set up a territory. They're hunters, predators and right now we are being hunted," stated Wil.

"Fuck! I don't want to die out here man. Why the fuck did I come on this stupid trip? I just wanted some time with Mary. Fuck me fuck me what are we going to do?"

Vanessa stepped forward and slapped Tom around the face. "You need to calm down!" she told him. "That's not helping."

Wil stepped between the two of them. "Get some sleep, those on watch keep your backs to the fire so your eyes stay adjusted to the dark and keep that fire built up. We can get through this if we stick together."

They all stared at each other in silence, fear on all their faces. John added more wood to the fire, Mary and Tom turned and went to their tent. Dave looked over at his friend and they settled in for the first watch. Rochelle stood at Wil's side took hold of his arm and nodded towards their tent.

Wil looked at his sister and handed her his bow. "Do you remember how to use this?"

She nodded, leaning in she kissed her brother on the cheek. "I remember." She moved away and settled in for a long night. In the distance the Kray-loth moved in the shadows, the bright light keeping it from attacking. In the distance came a howl, the creature turned its head and moved off to where it dropped its kill.

Chapter Seven

Sleep had come easy for Wil as it always did but his dreams were troubled. Images ran through his mind of the Mojave in the arena preparing for battle, all the different creatures held in the cells. These creatures had been taken as part of a rite of passage for the Mojave to do combat with, giving the Mojave the right to be called a warrior. They would choose the creature and the Mojave warriors would have to defeat them in hand-to-hand combat.

Wil tossed and turned in his sleep. He was now walking down a grey stone corridor; steel barred doors were set every few meters apart. Water dripped from the stone ceiling and he could hear the cries and sound of the creatures held within the cells. He looked down at his hand but the hand wasn't his. It was scaled and four fingered. Wil stopped and drew the sword from the scabbard on his hip, lifting it he looked at his reflection. Silted eyes stared back at him, his face was scaled and reptilian. A huge ape-like creature slammed into the cell door, reaching out with a clawed hand the beast was around nine feet tall, its fur grey. Two huge tusks protruded from beneath its bottom lip. The creature stepped back from the cell door dropping to all fours and ambled to the back of its cell. Wil stood looking at the creature as it stared back with murderous intent.

He moved on to the next cell. This one held a serpent-like creature which dragged itself on two powerful arms, it hissed at Wil as he walked past. Wil stopped at the next cell and stared into the darkness, the Kray-loth jumped forward, smashing into the cell door. Dust fell from the celling as the Kray-loth backed away, Wil's sword came up, pointing at the beast.

The image changed again. He found himself walking into the arena, looking left and right at the other Mojave warriors. The arena was packed as the Mojave spectators watched the young warriors enter, they were all armed with sword, axe or spear. The battle horn sounded followed by the sound of metal chains being lifted. A huge cheer rose up from the gathered crowd. At the other end of the arena two huge doors opened and out came the Kray-loth and it advanced on the warriors.

Wil, eyes flared open, his dreams had been of the alien world and the combat in the arena. Seeing again the Kray-loth trying to defend itself from the Mojave, he had seen again the awesome power in the Kray-loth, able to kill with one swipe of its murderous talons. Yet the Kray-loth wasn't evil, it was just an animal trying to defend itself. He rubbed at his eyes, they felt gritty, his dreams had left him feeling anxious. Could he get his friends to safety? Could they out run the Kray-loth?

Wil left his tent, the dawn light just starting to come through. Mary and Tom sat with their backs to the fire. Tom looked at his friend and nodded a greeting. "I'm going to scout around and see what I can find. I'll see if I can find any tracks."

Tom Grabbed Wil's arm. "Be careful, without you we're all dead."

Wil picked up his bow and moved off in the direction where Brad had been killed. Sure enough, Wil found the scene of Brad's death. In the ground were tracks, huge three toed paw prints, twice the size of a human hand. Wil knelt down and tried to dig his fingers into the same depth but barely marked the earth. The tracks moved off to the north, away from the camp. Wil followed them for a short distance just to see if the creature had circled around them. Still, they headed north and so did the blood trail. Wil heard raised voices coming from the campsite, he turned and ran back.

A full-blown argument was well under way. Vanessa was shouting at John. "Wil told us all to stay here and your stupid friend has gone to try and find that ship."

"It's not like I told him to go!" exclaimed John.

"What the hell is going on?" demanded Wil.

"Smithy took off to try and find the ship. All he kept talking about was how rich we could be if we took evidence back of alien life."

Wil cursed under his breath. "Vanessa, you take the others and head for the cabin. That thing's tracks go north; the cabin is to the east. I'll go after Smithy."

"Like hell you will!" Rochelle interrupted. "You said, we all need to stick together! Why should you risk yourself? Stay with us."

Wil took hold of Rochelle's hand. "Babe, I lost Brad. I'm not going to lose anyone else. Nessa knows the way from here, she'll get you there. Leave the tents, only take food and essentials. Get to the cabin. If you get there before I catch up get on the radio and call for help." Wil let go of Rochelle's hand and moved off in search of Dave.

Mary moved to Vanessa's side. "Nessa, what do we do?" she asked looking at the other woman.

"You heard him, we move."

Tom looked at Rochelle. "He'll be back, he's the toughest son of a bitch I know."

Wil was at an easy run heading back towards the crash site. No one knew how long Dave had been gone. Wil hoped to catch up with him before he got to the ship and turn him around and re-join the others, and hoped the Kray-loth was nowhere near. Dave stood open mouthed at the crashed spaceship, taking out his phone he started to take pictures of the outside. He saw the hole in the ship that Wil had mentioned. Climbing up, he entered the ship using the light on his phone as a torch, it was just as Wil had told them. He stumbled his way through to the flight deck and saw what was left of the pilot's body. The smell hit him and he gagged. "What the fuck is that?" he said out loud, taking more pictures. Scanning around he saw the strange hand print that Wil had described and placed his own hand in the recess. Nothing happened. "Busted," he said out loud.

A loud noise from outside the ship caused him to jump and he dropped his phone. It landed in the remains of the pilot. "Fuck me! That's all I need, dead alien guts on my phone." Dave retrieved his phone and gagged as he cleaned it off. Hearing a noise again he turned and moved back to exit the ship. As he reached the hole in the ship's side he stopped to look around, movement in the tree line caught his eye. He squinted, unsure what he was looking at. Wil was crouched down, barely visible waving his arm and pointing towards him. "Hey Wil, this shit is unreal we'll be famous." The sound of metal bending caused Dave to turn round. There stood upon the ship was the Kray-loth. It lashed out towards him but Dave stumbled and fell from the ship, landing hard on the floor. The air exploding from his lungs, he tried to rise and run but his legs were shaking. He couldn't call out as there was no air in his body to make a sound. Dave stumbled forward tripping once more, then he heard a loud thud and knew that the Kray-loth had landed behind him.

Sucking in a deep breath he started to run to where he had seen Wil hiding. He could hear the pounding of the Kray-loth gaining on him. He glanced back, the Kray-loth was almost on him. "If I can make it to the trees and Wil, I'll be fine," he thought. Pain lanced through his back, he saw the ground coming towards his face. He heard a terrible scream and the world went black. Wil watched in horror as the Kray-loth ripped into Dave. One slash from its razor-sharp talons had taken him down, opening up his back. The beast's huge maw snapping shut over his head and decapitating in one bite. The creature stood looking around, sniffing the air than started to feed. Wil could hear the crunching of bone as it fed.

Slowly and quietly, he slipped away from the feeding beast, once he knew he was clear, Wil picked up the pace. It had taken him thirty minutes to track Dave back to the ship. Vanessa would push the others to reach the cabin, checking his watch and keeping at his pace Wil estimated he was around forty-five minutes behind his friends. The howl came from behind him, the noise making his blood run cold. The answering howl came from just up ahead. Wil froze, he was heading into open country, no tree cover, just rolling hills. He would be easy prey for these creatures. Cursing, Wil changed direction. "Looks like it's the long way round," he said to himself.

Vanessa kept looking behind for any signs of her brother. She looked at Rochelle giving a reassuring smile. "Keep moving guys, we need to get to the cabin."

Rochelle looked at Vanessa. "What about Wil? What if those things are hunting him?"

"Don't worry about Wil, he's the best. If anyone can survive this it's him."

"Right, Ness," said Tom.

"He's right don't worry about Wil. Dad taught him well. If they are after him Wil knows how to stay hidden. We need to keep up the pace."

Mary dropped her pack to the ground. "Vanessa can we please just rest for a while, it feels like we've been walking forever."

Vanessa looked back in the direction they came from, she looked at her watch. "Okay, we'll take a ten-minute break. Have a drink, not too much or you'll get a stitch, Stay stood up don't let the lactic acid build up in your legs. I'm just going to head back and take a look and see if I can see any sign of Wil."

As Vanessa moved off John came over to Tom. "Do you know the way to this cabin?" he said in a low voice.

Tom looked at him. "No, why?"

John took him by the arm away from the others.

"What if they don't come back? what if those things get Wil and Nessa? We'll be out here with nowhere to go."

John was spun round and a hand slapped him across the face. Rochelle stood there, her eyes blazing with anger. "Shut up John! You heard Vanessa. Wil knows this place like the back of his hand. He'll come back with Vanessa, you'll see."

Tom walked past pushing his shoulder into John. "Brad was right about you John. You're a dick."

"Fuck you, Tom. In fact, fuck all of you!" snapped John. "I'm planning on surviving this in any way I can, if it means that we have to leave those two behind and find this cabin then that's what I'll do."

Rochelle took a step forward and looked him dead in the eyes. "You really are a piece of shit John. What does Nessa see in you, she deserves so much better."

John took a step back. "What, like good old Brad? If he were still alive, he'd be welcome to her?"

Tom ran forward pushing John in the chest double handed causing John to fall to the floor. Tom leant over him. "Brad was worth ten times more than you, and if he was stood here, he wouldn't be thinking of leaving anyone behind."

Mary came to Tom's side and led him away. "He's not worth it," she told him.

Vanessa stood looking at their back trail, she couldn't see any sign of her brother. Fear touched her. What if Wil didn't make it back? Was she strong enough to get the others through this? Every fibre of her wanted to go and look for him. She took a deep calming breath, turned and headed back towards the others.

It was only the answering howl from the other Kray-loth that had stopped Wil running directly into the beast. Wil had been forced back towards the ship. In his escape he ran down a small game trail and paused scouting around. He came across some deer droppings that were relatively fresh. Taking a handful he smeared them over his clothes then quickly climbed a tree and settled in. Keeping very still, hidden by the thick foliage Wil waited. He didn't need to wait long, the Kray-loth came crashing through the trees crushing small saplings in its path. The beast came to a stop suddenly and started to sniff the air. Wil's heart was pounding. Slowly he slid his hand towards his hunting knife. The creature stood for what seemed an eternity then came the god-awful howl again. The creature set off again answering its mate. Wil dropped from the tree, as soon as his legs hit the ground he was sprinting. The only thing that would save him now was to put as much distance between him and the Kray-loth.

As Vanessa and the others came to the top of the hill, they could see the welcome sight of the cabin in the bottom of the glen. It was a simple structure, one storey high made of pine. It had two bedrooms, a living area and a kitchen. The cabin had been built by Angus and his father years ago. They had installed an aqua pump to a nearby well that had given the cabin running water and a small generator for power that was housed in a small outbuilding to keep the noise down. While the generator was being installed Angus had used old oil burning lanterns for light. At one end of the cabin stood the stone chimney. Vanessa and her brother had spent so many years coming here, but this was the first time she had been here without her father and would give anything to have him here now.

Vanessa paused. Something wasn't right. Smoke was already coming from the chimney. Amanda came along the side of her. "What's wrong?" she asked.

"Look down there," said Vanessa pointing. "There's smoke coming from the chimney. There's no way Wil could have beaten us here."

"So, who's in there?" asked Amanda.

Vanessa shrugged. "Let's find out."

They all set off down to the cabin. As they got closer Vanessa saw a quad at the side of the cabin and noticed the dried blood down the side. The door opened and Angus emerged carrying a shotgun. He looked at the group of people approaching and shook his head a look of sorrow on his face. Vanessa ran forward and hugged him. "Angus, what are you doing up here?"

"Sweet Mary, Mother of God, Vanessa! I was hoping you wouldn't come. Quick, get inside. Hurry!"

As they entered the cabin Vanessa saw Morag laid asleep on the sofa, a bloody bandage covering her leg.

"My god Angus! What happened?" Angus took Vanessa by the arm and led her away from the others.

"We were out enjoying the warm weather a couple of days ago. We took the quad out and thought we'd come and get the cabin ready for you and Wil but something attacked us. It moved so quick, we barely got away, it caught Morag on the leg. She's lost a lot of blood. I don't know how long she'll last, the wound won't close. It's as if there's something in her blood that keeps the wound bleeding."

"The same thing attacked us last night," she told him. "It killed one of our friends. Wil's out there now trying to find one of us who wondered off back to the crash site."

"What crash site?" asked Angus.

Vanessa looked at Angus. "While Wil was out setting rabbit snares he came upon a crashed spaceship in the woods, a short distance from the second campsite. He went inside, and somehow, he interfaced with the ship's computer memories. It showed him what was out there. He found that blonde haired woman hiding inside the ship, those things attacked her and her friends she managed to escape."

"Wil's out there with those things? Christ! They keep coming back here. I think I wounded one but I can't be sure, and I'm nearly out of ammo."

John walked over to Angus. "You have a quad and a shotgun, you could go out and look for Wil or go and get help," he said his voice hopeful.

Angus looked the man square in the eyes. "Can't do that lad. When that beasty attacked us, it severed the fuel line, that quad is useless."

"But you have a gun," said Tom joining the conversation. "We can't just sit here and wait for those things to come back."

"He's right," said John. "We should take the gun and try and get back to the farm."

"No way," said Tom. "We need to find Wil." A small argument broke out between the two men.

Angus raised his voice. "Look lads, that beast is out there and even if that quad worked the noise of the engine would only attract that thing to you."

Rochelle stepped forward. "Wil's out there, someone has to go and help him." Mary and Amanda nodded their agreement.

Angus took a deep breath. "Looks lassie, if Wil is out there, he's better off on his own. His father and I taught him well. Any of you would only get in his way. He knows how to avoid danger and stay out of sight. If any of us have a chance it's him."

The group stood in silence then a moan came from the sleeping Morag. "Angus, where are you?"

"I'm here my love, don't worry. Look who's here."

Vanessa came into view. Morag looked at the young girl and started to sob. "Oh, sweet Jesus. Why are you here? You have to get away!"

Vanessa leant down and kissed her forehead. "It's okay. Shhh, just lay there and be still."

Morag reached out her hand and placed it on Vanessa's cheek. "You have to get away child. So young so beautiful," said Morag stroking Vanessa's hair. "Angus get them away from here, you have to."

Angus took hold of her hand. "Shhh, now rest my love." He leant forward and kissed her.

Morag smiled at him. "I love you," she told him.

"And I you, lass."

Morag took in a deep shuddering breath, her hand went limp. Angus looked down at her. Morag's dead eyes stared back at him. A tear rolled down his cheek gently. He closed his wife's eyes. "My god woman. I'm sorry, I failed you." Vanessa put her hand on his shoulder, tears running down her face. Angus covered her with a blanket.

Vanessa let out a sob as Angus turned to her. "She loved you like a daughter lass. Take heart, know she's at peace." Turning back and taking hold of his wife's hand, "Oh my sweet Morag, I love you. Rest now my beauty. Vanessa, pass me a bottle of whisky."

Vanessa went to a wooden cabinet near the fireplace. Opening it, she passed him the bottle, resting her hand on his shoulder. Angus removed the top off the bottle and took a big long drink. "To you my love," he said. "Heaven now has one more angel."

The door burst open, Angus swung the gun around to see Wil stood there. Before anyone could say anything, Rochelle was in Wil's arms, sobbing openly. "Wil, thank God you're okay," she said, pulling back from him. "You stink, what happened?"

The others gathered round. "I got to the crash site but one of those things was already tracking him. I tried to warn him but it was waiting on top of the ship. As he came out it pounced. So I knew while it had him I could make my escape."

"Wait!" shouted John. "You just let it kill Smithy? You just left him there?"

Wil looked at John. "I'm sorry but I had no choice. If I'd have shouted or moved then I wouldn't be here. He was dead the moment he left the campsite."

John turned and stormed off to the back of the cabin. Wil felt all eyes on him. "They're fast. I started after you guys but one of them was in front of me. I had to turn back and try to hide from them, hence the smell," he gestured to smeared deer droppings down the front of his shirt.

John pushed his way forward. "What the fuck is that bow for? Why didn't you try to help him?"

A hand fell on John's shoulder. "That bow wouldn't do much damage to that thing lad," said Angus stepping past John and embracing Wil. "God's boy, it's good to see you!"

Wil smiled at his friend. "You've seen them up close?" he asked Angus.

"Aye, lad, big fuckers aren't they? I think I wounded one but my ammo is low. They'll be back tonight testing to see if I'm still here. They're smart lad, they keep out of firing distance."

Wil looked over and saw Morag's body on the couch looking back at Angus. "When?" he asked, sadness in his voice.

Angus dropped his head. "Just before you got here lad, I'm surprised she lasted as long as she did. That damn wound on her leg just wouldn't stop bleeding, it's like there's something in her blood that stopped the blood from clotting. She slowly bled to death over three days. I've been stuck here not able to do anything."

"What about the radio?" asked Tom. "Why haven't you used it and gotten help?"

"No signal down in the glen lad. We need higher ground."

"What do you mean no signal? Wil, you said we could call for help from here!"

Tom looked at his friend panic sounding in his voice. "You can lad, but you'll have to go out there to the top of that hill or higher to get a signal," said Angus laying a calming hand on Tom's shoulder.

"Out there!" exclaimed John. "With those things running around? Fuck that! No way, man! You can count me out."

Vanessa looked over at the panic on his face and shook her head. "I guess we can count you out of most things," she said.

"Too right you can!" he replied, not hiding his shame. An argument broke out between them, Angus held up his hand for silence.

"Wil and I can go, we're the only ones that could do it anyway."

Rochelle stepped in front of Wil. "Oh no! He's just got back, no one is taking him away from me again."

Mary took her by the hand. "Someone has to try," she said. Rochelle could see the look of hope on her face and sighed.

A howl broke the tension. Angus ran to the door. The two black creatures were slowly moving towards the cabin. He swore. "Clever bastards, they know the range of the gun. Look, see how they're hanging back, testing us, waiting to see if we make a mistake."

Vanessa moved to the window. "Look, the one on the right seems to be limping."

A harsh laugh came from Angus. "I told you I got one of those bastards!"

"So why aren't they attacking?" asked Tom.

"I told you lad they keep testing. When I wounded it, they seemed to be more cautious about attacking."

Wil took a deep breath. "They know we're here so someone has to go for help and it should be me."

"No!" cried Rochelle. "What if they see you? They'll

come after you and kill you."

Wil walked to her. "It has to be me!" he told her. "I know the terrain and I'm the fastest."

Vanessa moved to Wil's side looking at Rochelle. "Someone has to go. We only have a few days of food left and then they'll just starve us out. Wil is our best chance to survive this."

Tears brimmed in Rochelle's eyes, taking Wil's hand she kissed it. "Come back to me," she pleaded.

Wil lent in and kissed her. "Always," he whispered. He looked up at his friends. "I need you to create some kind of distraction, something that will keep them both focused on this place and not on me."

"I'll take care of that lad," said Angus. "Where are you heading for?"

"I'll go to the top of the gorge, it's the highest point. Best chance we have of getting a signal. Plus, I can see if one of those things has followed me."

"That's a fair distance lad," Angus replied. "But you're right it's the best chance for a clean signal." Wil walked to the fireplace where a large hunting knife had been mounted on the wall. Removing his own knife, he strapped on the larger one and handed his knife to his sister.

"Take this, you may need it."

Grabbing his bow and the radio he moved to the rear of the cabin and placed his hand on the door handle. "When you're ready Angus," he said. Angus opened the door and stepped out in plain sight of the creatures. Instantly they both fixed their gaze on him.

"Now Wil!" shouted Vanessa. Wil set off running to

get to higher ground, cutting left towards the small grove of trees. This would keep him from sight. The breeze was at his back, this would help keep his scent away from the Kray-loth. It would take Wil nearly an hour at this pace to reach the bottom of the gorge, then he had to climb fifty feet to the top. The climb in good light was dangerous and in fading light would be deadly. Wil looked up at the afternoon sun. "I only have a few hours of good light left," he said aloud. Wil increased his pace. Back at the cabin the rest watched as Angus played decoy, giving Wil time get away in hope he can call for help.

Chapter Eight

Angus stepped out further from the doorway. "What are you doing?" asked Tom, sticking his head out of the door.

Angus kept moving forward. "I'm making sure that those things stay focused on me," he said without looking back. Vanessa and Amanda watched from the window as Angus moved further away from the safety of the cabin.

John joined Tom at the door, a look of horror on his face as Angus stepped out even further. "Why are they just waiting there? Why hunt us? What have we done to them?" asked Amanda.

"We've done nothing," said Vanessa. "We're just easy prey. Those things have set up a territory and we're trespassing."

"These fuckers are moving!" shouted Angus. "Something's not right, the wounded one is heading away." Angus stuck his finger in his mouth and held it in the air. "The wind's changed, it has Wil's scent."

"No!" screamed Rochelle. "Someone has to go warn him, they'll kill him!"

"You lad, what's your name?" snapped Angus pointing a finger towards Tom.

"It's Tom," he replied, his voice shaking.

"Come over here Tom. Keep an eye on that thing out there, tell me if it moves. You!" said Angus pointing at

John. "Come out as well."

"Why? What for?" asked John nervously.

"Because you're going to keep that beasty looking at you while I go and help young Wil."

"What? How?" said John with panic in his voice.

Angus spun on him. "Look, all of you have to get me a head start. The wind is blowing straight towards that thing, as soon as I make a run for Wil that thing will be after me. You all need to come outside and create as much scent as possible, giving me time to get to Wil."

The look of horror on John's face was apparent. "Out there? With that thing? Are you crazy?" he said.

Angus looked at them all and it showed from his expression that this was no joke. "I, lad, I'm afraid so," he replied.

Vanessa walked past him out on to the open ground. "He's right, we need to keep that thing here. Its Wil's only chance. We'll keep it busy Angus, you go help Wil."

Rochelle moved to stand with her. The Kray-loth seeing the movement started to pace back and forth. Tom and John came out, armed with knives from the kitchen, followed by Amanda and Mary. The Kray-loth stood as their scent filled its nostrils, its muscles quivered with the rich sent of their flesh making its mouth salivate.

Vanessa looked back towards the cabin. "Okay Angus, we have its attention. Go!" she called out. Angus ran through the cabin and slipped out the back, gun in hand and set off after Wil.

Vanessa looked at her friends, panic on all their faces. "Okay, spread out," she told them. "Don't go too far and expose yourself too much. We just need to keep its attention. If it moves, we move back to the cabin."

The Kray-loth looked down at the growing number of people, spoilt for choice on which one to attack. It started to move round in circles, gauging the distance between each one of them. "What's it doing, Nessa?" shouted Tom. "Do we go back inside?"

"Not yet, we need to give Angus more time," she replied. "John, don't go so far out. Stay within running distance of the cabin."

"Don't worry, I won't," came his answer.

Amanda grabbed Mary by the arm. "If we can reach that hill over there, we could make a run for it back to the farm and call for help."

Tom who was stood ten feet away shouted over, "No, that's a real bad idea. Wil is a fitness freak and even he wouldn't chance it."

Amanda started to pull Mary further away. "Look that thing is more interested in the others. We can make a run for it and escape."

Mary started to follow her. Tom looked over at his girlfriend. "You won't make it. Wil and Angus are our best chance!" he told them.

Amanda pulled Mary by the arm harder this time. "I'm not waiting around here while Wil is being hunted down by that thing. Come on," she said and set off at a run, instinctively Mary followed.

Tom couldn't believe what he was seeing. "Mary, come back!" he shouted but it was too late, Amanda and Mary were sprinting away from the cabin. The Kray-loth seeing movement instantly gave chase. Vanessa and the others watched in horror as the creature closed in on the two fleeing women. The Kray-loth soon closed the distance on the two women, with one slash of its talons Mary was torn in half. The beast took one huge leap forward and Amanda was pinned to the floor. The Kray-loth opened its mouth and with one bite Amanda's head disappeared, her body was flung ten feet in the air as the Kray-loth reared its head.

Tom seeing his girlfriend struck down, ran forward, all fear gone. Armed with a long kitchen knife he ran towards the Kray-loth screaming Mary's name at the top of his lungs. The Kray-loth turned to meet its attacker. It jumped forward slashing at Tom's stomach which disembowelled him. Tom fell to his knees, he looked down to see his entrails spilling to the floor. He blinked in disbelief. He looked up into the black eyes of the Kray-loth then darkness engulfed him.

As Tom's body hit the floor the Kray-loth looked over at the remaining people. It let out a howl and moved towards them. Vanessa grabbed Rochelle by the arm. "Get back inside! Quickly!" she shouted, dragging her towards the cabin. Frantically they both ran back towards safety as Vanessa's hand curled round the door handle. Rochelle was cannoned into her, the two women hit the floor as John pushed them out of the way and disappeared inside.

Quickly Vanessa got to her feet and helped Rochelle up and slammed the door shut. She turned towards John who stood, knife in hand. "You made it," he said, sheepishly walking forward.

She slapped him round the face. "No thanks to you," she said through gritted teeth. "What the hell was that out there?"

John backed away from the angry woman. "I was just running too fast, I couldn't stop!" he stammered. A loud thud came from the door followed by a loud sniffing sound. Vanessa held her finger to her lips calling for them to be quiet. Slowly they backed into the kitchen.

Wil's legs were burning and his muscles ached. He had not eaten all day and he was tiring. He emerged from the tree line, finally he had reached the bottom of the gorge. Shouldering his bow and the radio he started the climb, loose stone made it treacherous. To attempt this without climbing gear was crazy but the lives of his sister and the others depended on him. The first twenty feet of the climb wasn't too hard, he had slipped a couple of times, only his strength saving him from falling. Now at thirty-five feet the climb was hard. His hands ached, his fingers were cramping and the light was fading. He paused on a small outcrop to catch his breath, then he heard the growl that made his blood run cold.

One of the Kray-loth had followed him and was at the bottom of the gorge looking up at him. The Kray-loth moved forward and started to climb, its huge claws digging into the stone. Wil looked up at the last fifteen feet — taking a deep breath he started the last of the climb.

Twice more he slipped, telling himself not to look back, just keep moving. He reached out with his right hand, and gripped the top, he swung his left arm up and with one massive heave pulled himself over the top. Looking down the Kray-loth had reached the outcrop. Quickly Wil notched an arrow to his bow, drew in a breath and let fly the arrow. It plunged into the shoulder of the advancing beast but still it climbed. Wil loosed arrow after arrow, hoping to dislodge the monster that was closing in on him. Taking a deep calming breath Wil remembered his father's teachings. "Think about your opponent, look for the weakness then take advantage of that weakness. It could be the difference between losing and winning."

Wil reached back, only two arrows left. Notching one he took aim, as he let out his breath, he loosed the arrow. A cry of pain came from the Kray-loth as the arrow burred itself in its right eye, the beast slipped and almost fell, its claws digging into the rock face. Wil took the last arrow and took aim, the Kray-loth had slipped back to the outcrop but was advancing again. Wil took his shot the arrow flying for the left eye. The Kray-loth turned its head at the last second, the arrow thudding into its shoulder. Wil's heart sank. Dropping his bow, he drew the knife at his side. "I'll take you with me you bastard!" he shouted. "Come and get me!" A gunshot echoed followed by another, then another. Wil looked down, Angus was stood some fifteen feet below the beast. Another shot sounded out. To Wil's horror the Kray-loth turned and dove towards its attacker. Angus saw the beast turn and dive towards him. Time seemed to slow down, his life playing out before his eyes; his years on the farm, enrolment into the army, meeting Morag, meeting Alex, their time away in the Middle East, his regiment being captured, and his quick thinking which saved his life, all came flooding forward. Now he had the chance to pay his friend back. Angus brought the gun to his shoulder, took aim and fired.

The shot took the Kray-loth in the open mouth, exiting through the back of its head. Its body hit Angus and they fell. Wil watched the scene with horror as both of them hit the floor. "No!" cried Wil. He was now torn between going down to Angus or calling for help. Turning he picked up the radio and flipped the switch. "Mayday, mayday, mayday, is anyone receiving?" He released the trigger, the sound of static came over the radio. Again, he called for help. "Mayday, mayday, mayday, is anyone receiving, please?" Releasing the trigger once more static again.

Wil was about to press when a voice came through. "Roger, we receive you. What's your mayday?"

Wil felt a rush of hope sweep through his body. "My name is Wil Jameson, I'm at the McDougal cabin north of the McDougal farm. We've been attacked by some kind of creature. We have three of our party dead and six more in danger. We need help!"

The voice from the radio came back an edge of suspicion in his voice. "You do know that this channel is for emergencies only, not some drunken joke?"

Wil pressed the button. "What's your name?" he asked.

"My name is Officer Matt Symes of the mountain rescue. Why?" he asked.

Wil's voice was cold. "Because, Officer Matt Symes, if I survive this, I'm going to come find you and I'm going to break every bone in your body. So do me a favour put the bar of chocolate, down get off your arse and come and help save us! I'll repeat my earlier message, we have three people dead and another six in great danger. We've been attacked by a fucking alien. If you still don't believe me, bring the fucking police with you, and arrest me for wasting your time, but tell them to bring as many fucking guns as they can get because they'll need them to protect you if my sister and friends are dead when I get back to them."

Wil didn't wait for the answer, he tossed the radio aside and quickly made his way down to Angus. Wil looked down on his friends broken body, tears forming in his eyes. The Kray-loth was some six feet away, blood pouring from its open mouth. Kneeling he felt for a pulse. Angus opened his eyes. "Got the son of a bitch," he said weakly.

"Don't move Angus," said Wil. "I'll get you back to the cabin."

Angus raised his hand. "No lad, I'm done for."

Wil shook his head. "No please, Angus!" he pleaded. "I can't lose you."

Angus gripped Wil's arm. "You have to go save your sister," he said weakly. "Take the gun and go boy, they need you."

"No!" cried Wil. "I won't leave you here to die."

Angus coughed, blood spilling from his mouth. He took a deep calming breath. "You can't save me lad but you can save the others now go."

Wil picked up the gun then looked back at his dying friend. "I love you Angus, like a father. I always will." He turned on his heels and set off at a run, tears flowed from Angus.

"I love you too, my bonny lad." He coughed and a

119

spasm of pain shot through his body. Angus looked up at the darkening sky. "I paid you back Alex," he said weakly. "I saved the lad." Pain flared again through his body, his breathing was becoming more ragged now. Between breaths he whispered, "Morag my love, you've come for me. You look so beautiful." He lifted his hand towards the sky and smiled. Morag stood above him dressed in white, she held her hand towards him her fingertips touching his. Angus closed his eyes, all pain disappearing.

"Come my love," she told him. "Come and know peace." His hand dropped to the ground, Angus took one final breath and was gone.

The light was fading, making it harder for Wil. If he tripped on a rock or a hidden root, he could twist his ankle or worse, break it. He had seen the power of the Kray-loth as it climbed the rock face, its massive talons gripping the rock, and the speed at which it had climbed up after him. If it wasn't for Angus, he knew he would now be dead. Sorrow hit him as he recalled the beast turning and diving towards his friend, its massive body colliding with Angus. Now his sister and the others were trapped inside a wooden cabin with one of those beasts waiting for them.

Rochelle ducked down from the small window at the front of the cabin. "It's coming!" she said, panic in her voice.

Vanessa ran forward. "Help me move some of the furniture. We need to barricade the door."

The sound of creaking wood came from outside as the Kray-loth stepped onto the porch. Vanessa froze holding her finger to her lips, gesturing for silence. From the door they could hear the Kray-loth taking in deep breaths as it tried to scent them. Vanessa slowly moved away from the door followed by Rochelle. The front wall of the cabin shook as the Kray-loth hammered its shoulder into it.

Rochelle and Vanessa moved past the still form of John who was now rooted to the spot with fear. He was mumbling to himself, "It's not real, it's not real."

Vanessa took his hand whispering, "Come on, we have to move to the back of the cabin."

John turned his gaze from the door, to Vanessa. "It's not real," he whispered. Sounds of wood being scratched came from the side of the cabin as the Kray-loth made its way towards the rear.

Letting go of John's hand Vanessa turned to Rochelle. "It's moving round the back, we have to block the back door?"

Rochelle nodded and the two women moved into the kitchen. "John, help us," whispered Rochelle. All colour had drained from John's face, his breathing increasing. "John," she whispered again. "Please help us."

John's eyes widened as the scratching of wood grew louder. "It's not real," he said again, this time his voice rising. Vanessa tried to shush him but the fear had taken over and John was now in full panic. "It's not real," he said again, this time shouting.

Rochelle rushed forward grabbing hold of his hand. "John be quiet," she pleaded.

"It's not real!" he screamed in her face, pushing her to the ground.

Vanessa ran forward and slapped him across the face. "Be quiet you fool!"

John pushed her to one side and ran for the door. "It's not real!" he screamed again, now in full hysterics. John wrenched open the door and ran outside. "It's not real!" he shouted once more.

Vanessa ran to the door. "John, come back inside!" she pleaded, but he didn't hear her calling to him. A low growl from behind cut through John's insanity. Slowly he turned to look directly into the black eyes of the nightmare beast. He now stood face to face with the Kray-loth.

"You're not real!" he screamed at the top of his voice. "You're not fucking real!" Vanessa had taken a few steps away from the safety of the doorway just as the beast had come into view. The Kray-loth let out a hideous cry and with one swipe of it paw opened John from throat to groin.

Vanessa screamed out as John's body hit the floor, the Kray-loth turned and charged. Vanessa slammed the door shut only to be knocked off her feet and cannoned into Rochelle as the door smashed open. Dazed she looked up the Kray-loth stood in the doorway, its massive shoulders preventing access through the door. Frantically the beast snapped at the door frame trying to get inside. Wil came through the small grove of trees, the cabin came into view and so did the nightmare that was happening. The Kray-loth was squeezing through the rear door. Wil ran down towards the monster, moving in close he aimed the gun and fired. The shot hit the creature in the hind leg on its knee joint, a screech of pain came from the Kray-loth. It turned to meet its attacker but as it turned its head Wil levelled the gun, aiming directly at the open mouth and fired. Click! The gun was empty. With a backhanded swing of its massive front leg, it hit Wil in the chest, sending him flying through the air, crashing into the small wood store. The creature tried to advance and let out a howl of pain and looked back at its damaged leg. Slowly the creature advanced towards its attacker, Wil hit the ground hard all breath knocked from his body. He lay on his back winded, trying to take in deep breaths. He pushed his arms under himself and tried to rise on unsteady legs but fell to his knees.

Panic set in as the Kray-loth advanced towards him, closer and closer it came. Wil struggled to rise as the beast came closer still. Vanessa ran from behind and with a scream of frustration she plunged Wil's hunting knife deep in the side of the creature's neck. The Kray-loth turned on its new attacker, snapping its powerful jaws towards Vanessa causing her to fall backwards. As she hit the floor, she tried to roll but pain lanced through her leg.

The Kray-loth snapped shut its jaw onto her leg and flung her through the air. Wil surged to his feet with the hunting knife in hand and swung with all his might, severing one of the Kray-loth's small arms. The Kray-loth stumbled back in pain, slashing out towards Wil who dived to his left. Scooping up the wood axe in his left hand he reversed the hunting knife, drew back his arm and threw it. The blade took the Kray-loth in the chest near the severed limb. Wil ran forward swinging the axe, opening a deep cut in its right leg.

The Kray-loth reeled back again, slashing at its

attacker only to miss. Wil dove under as the creature swung at him, rolling under the deadly talons coming up on his feet and running for the cabin. Wil ran as fast as he could not looking back. As he entered the cabin, he found Rochelle crouched under the table hugging her knees. She screamed as he came through the broken door. "Are you hurt? Can you move?" he asked. She nodded. Wil took her by the arm pulling her to her feet. "We have to trap it in here and burn the place down while its inside."

"How do we do that?" she asked. "Where's Nessa?"

Wil could hear the fear in her voice. "Out there," he told her. "Alive, I think. Start moving that stuff away from the front door, that thing can't get through the door so easy. I'll slow it down you clear our exit and we can kill this thing."

"I can't!" cried Rochelle.

"Yes, you can, or we all die!" snapped Wil. He grabbed one of the oil lanterns from the wall and smashed it on the kitchen floor. Looking at Rochelle, he told her, "We can do this! Now, clear our exit!"

Rochelle frantically started to move the furniture away from the door, Wil, axe in hand, turned and grabbed two more of the oil lanterns smashing them. Then taking two bottles of whisky he stuffed a rag into each the necks of the bottles, then he focused on the doorway. The Kray-loth was slowly making its way forward, it seemed more cautious now, hesitant to rush forward and kill its victims. Slowly it reached the doorway.

There stood the man, defiant weapon in hand ready to fight. With a growl it moved forward. Wil swung the axe, the Kray-loth pulled back then advanced. Again, Wil jumped forward swinging a murderous arc with the axe, the Kray-loth pulled back again.

"Wil, I have the door open. Come on!" Rochelle called out.

"Not yet, we have to trap it inside." He turned to look at the panicked woman. "Pick up the bottles and light the rags," he told her, tossing her a lighter from his pocket.

As he turned his head the Kray-loth surged forward while the man was distracted momentary, its huge frame getting stuck in the doorway. For a few seconds the frame held the monster in place, then the sound of splintering wood caused Wil to turn back as the Kray-loth busted in. With a double handed grip on the axe Wil drew it back over his head and threw it at the advancing creature. The axe hit the Kray-loth in the shoulder causing it to lose its balance, it slipped in the oil. Wil turned, grabbing one of the bottles from Rochelle, throwing it past the Kray-loth which smashed on the floor. Instantly flame took hold, igniting the whisky and the oil from the lanterns.

Turning on his heel, Wil made for the door grabbing Rochelle and pushing her outside. He threw the second bottle, this one smashing on the Kray-loth's head. Flames picked up, instantly engulfing its body, spreading all around. The Kray-loth started to thrash. Wild cries of pain echoing as it burnt.

Outside Wil and Rochelle watched as the cabin burst into flames. The cries and howling were haunting as the flames grew bigger. "We did it!" shouted Rochelle. "Burn you bastard, burn!" The front door and part of the wall exploded outwards, knocking Rochelle backwards off of her feet. The Kray-loth ran head first into Wil, knocking him through the air. As he landed, he rolled to his back hitting one of the burning timbers. He rolled from the burning wood, the Kray-loth leapt forward and pinned him to the floor. Burnt and bloody it stood over him. The Kray-loth let out a howl, holding its head up to the night sky.

Seeing his only chance, the hunting knife he had thrown, was still embedded in its chest. Quickly he reached up, pulling the knife clear as the creature opened its mouth to snap its jaws on him. Wil drove the knife through the open mouth and up into its brain. The Kray-loth tried to move then slumped forward, its weight pinning Wil to the floor.

Wil laid on the ground breathing deeply, he heard Rochelle called out his name. With all his strength he pushed at the dead beast and rolled clear. Wil turned towards Rochelle, she was crying and crawling towards him. Reaching out he pulled her into an embrace. Movement from the Kray-loth caused Rochelle to scream. Wil, knife in hand, lunged for the beast, just missing Vanessa as she crawled into sight.

"I know I look rough but there's no need to kill me," she said weakly.

Wil jumped up. "You're alive!"

"Just," she said. "Had to save your arse again." She winced. "I think my leg is broken," she told him. Wil removed his top, tore it into strips and used it to bandage Vanessa's leg. Looking at her brother she asked, "Angus?"

Wil shook his head. "No, he sacrificed himself to save me. He killed the other one." Vanessa looked back